Erin framed his face with her hands and rested her face against his. "I'm here, Alec. For whatever you need. Always. I promise."

He sank fingers into her hair, holding her close and covering her face with achingly tender kisses. Desperate kisses. Kisses full of affection and emotion and words left unsaid. Words that hovered near the surface. Words she saw reflected in his azure eyes.

She felt the tremor that shook him, and her body answered with a quaking need and clamoring hunger. She held him tighter, angling her hips and shifting her legs, wishing she could climb inside him. Fill him. Give him all the love he'd been denied and had denied himself for too many years.

Dear Reader,

Soldier's Pregnancy Protocol is a story of second chances, both for me and for the characters. When I wrote the book originally, I had a blast filling the story with high adventure, daring feats and lots of nail-biting suspense. I was channeling Jack Bauer from *24* and packing as much action and tension in the book as I could. I loved writing it, because action scenes are my favorite to write. But the Romantic Suspense line was going through growing pains at the time, and the new vision for the line was for less suspense and more relationship. The book was rejected because it had too much suspense! So I stuck the book away but never forgot the story I loved. When it was a finalist in my local RWA chapter's contest, my new editor got the chance to read the first chapter and, lo and behold, she loved it! After the contest, I sent her the finished book, tweaked to have a bit more focus on the couple's relationship, and not only was *Soldier's Pregnancy Protocol* born, but a whole Black Ops Rescues miniseries!

I hope you enjoy *Soldier's Pregnancy Protocol*. Watch for Daniel's book, coming in August!

Happy reading,

Beth Cornelison

BETH CORNELISON

Soldier's Pregnancy Protocol

ROMANTIC
SUSPENSE

Recycling programs
for this product may
not exist in your area.

ISBN-13: 978-0-373-373-27779-7

SOLDIER'S PREGNANCY PROTOCOL

Copyright © 2012 by Beth Cornelison

www.Harlequin.com

Printed in U.S.A.

Books by Beth Cornelison

Harlequin Romantic Suspense

  Special Ops Bodyguard #1668
  Operation Baby Rescue #1677
†*Soldier's Pregnancy Protocol* #1709

Silhouette Romantic Suspense

  To Love, Honor and Defend #1362
  In Protective Custody #1422
  Danger at Her Door #1478
  Duty to Protect #1522
  Rancher's Redemption #1532
  Tall Dark Defender #1566
★*The Christmas Stranger* #1581
  Blackout at Christmas #1583
    "Stranded with the Bridesmaid"
★*The Bride's Bodyguard* #1630
  P.I. Daddy's Personal Mission #1632

★*The Prodigal Bride* #1646
★*The Bancroft Brides*
†*Black Ops Rescues*

★The Bancroft Brides
^Black Ops Rescues

Other titles by this author
  available in ebook format.

BETH CORNELISON

started writing stories as a child when she penned a tale about the adventures of her cat, Ajax. A Georgia native, she received her bachelor's degree in public relations from the University of Georgia. After working in public relations for a little more than a year, she moved with her husband to Louisiana, where she decided to pursue her love of writing fiction.

Since that first time, Beth has written many more stories of adventure and romantic suspense and has won numerous honors for her work, including a coveted Golden Heart Award in romantic suspense from Romance Writers of America. She is active on the board of directors for the North Louisiana Storytellers and Authors of Romance (NOLA STARS) and loves reading, traveling, *Peanuts'* Snoopy and spending downtime with her family.

She writes from her home in Louisiana, where she lives with her husband, one son and two cats who think they are people. Beth loves to hear from her readers. You can write to her at P.O. Box 5418, Bossier City, LA 71171 or visit her website at www.bethcornelison.com.

To Keyren Gerlach, who gave Alec and Erin new life!
I appreciate all you do.

Prologue

Without a sound, Alec Kincaid inched on his belly through the sticky black mud of the South American jungle until he had a clearer view of the Cessna awaiting takeoff from the small clearing. The acrid scent of jet fuel and jeep exhaust tinged the smell of rotting vegetation and the fragrance of the orchids blooming around his hiding place. His body ached from lying motionless for the past twelve hours, but his gut told him his efforts would soon pay off. In spades.

After ten years, working black ops for a counterterrorist team so secret the group didn't even have a name, Alec had learned to rely on his instincts and not much else. Except training. Except Daniel LeCroix, aka *Lafitte*.

He trusted his partner with his life. And had many times. Just this week.

In the past five years, Alec had lost count how many times he and Lafitte had relied on each other for survival in the murky world of espionage and counterterrorism.

Because of the risks they took, their rogue lifestyle, the

pirate code names they'd adopted seemed apropos. *Blackbeard and Lafitte.*

He clicked his tongue three times into his lip mic. *Three tangos.*

In his earpiece, he heard Daniel's reply, a short puff of air. *Affirmative.*

Alec sighted his AK-47 on the rebel fighters as they loaded boxes of weapons into the aircraft. But these drones were not his ultimate target. Intel indicated General Ramirez, the murderous leader of the rebel fighters, would be leaving on this flight.

If they netted Ramirez today, he and Daniel could be swilling rum with a couple senoritas on a beach in Acapulco by nightfall—Lafitte and Blackbeard savoring the spoils of a completed mission. Three years of mucking through mosquito-infested rain forests and living weeks at a time off grubs and stubborn determination had led to this moment.

Anticipation thrummed through Alec. His nerves jangled, but he didn't so much as draw a deep breath. Any movement, any noise could give away his position. He held his post without flinching, even when one of the deadliest spiders in Colombia dropped from an overhanging branch and crept up his arm. To his neck. Inside his mud-caked camo T-shirt…

His gut pitched. *Mother of Joe, he hated spiders!*

Through his headset, Daniel could probably hear the rapid fire of Alec's pulse as the arachnid skulked down his back.

The rumble of a motor cued him to an approaching jeep. Spider or not, Alec forced his focus to the new arrival, years of training kicking into high gear.

Daniel grunted. *See that?*

Alec puffed on the mike. *Affirmative.*

Daniel clicked twice. *Two more men.*

General Ramirez and a guard. Five tangos against the two of them. A cakewalk.

But foreboding rolled through Alec like a thundercloud. It didn't add up. Why wasn't the general better guarded? Alec held his breath as General Ramirez climbed from the jeep, shouting directions in Spanish to his men. With a low whine, the Cessna engine turned over, and the nose propeller spun.

Every muscle in Alec's body tensed. Ready.

All of his senses honed in on the scene before him. Waiting for the right moment...

Ramirez stepped away from the jeep, turned his back. Alec had a clear shot, but Uncle Sam wanted Ramirez taken alive. The general's guards were fair game, though. Alec curled his finger around the trigger of his assault rifle. Took aim. Prepared to charge the aircraft and kick some rebel ass.

But across the clearing, a blast of gunfire ripped from the jungle. Peppered the jeep, the Cessna. The aircraft exploded in a ball of flame and black smoke. The concussion shook the ground and reverberated in Alec's chest.

What the hell?

In his earpiece, he heard Daniel mutter the same expletive that popped in his mind.

Chaos erupted. Ramirez clutched his chest. Fell.

The rebels returned fire. Shooting blindly. Spraying the area with a hail of bullets.

Uniformed men, a rival militia force, surged from the line of trees.

Mud splattered, and the foliage hiding Alec shredded under the barrage of gunfire.

"Pull back! Abort!" he grated into his mic.

Daniel didn't respond.

"Copy, pirate? Abort!" Alec repeated as he shimmied backward through the black ooze, scrambled to his feet, and shook the nasty spider out of his shirt. Still crouched low, he wove through the maze of trees while three years of tedious undercover work went to hell in the clearing.

Where was Daniel, damn it? Why didn't he answer?

A helicopter buzzed low over the clearing. Suddenly the jungle teemed with enemy fighters.

Don't jeopardize the mission. If things go south, it's every man for himself. He and Daniel had sworn to abide by the agreement as they broke camp yesterday morning. But yesterday, Alec had arrogantly believed nothing could stop him and his partner from bringing the general in.

Sweat and mud stung Alec's eyes as he plowed through the dense rain forest. A bright green bird shrieked and took flight as Alec charged through the mist-shrouded jungle. He pressed on, despite stiff muscles and the encumbering weight of the black sludge he'd smeared on his skin for camouflage.

Daniel was as highly trained as Alec. His partner would be fine.

Alec glided through the rain forest like a jaguar, already mentally regrouping. Ramirez had been shot. If the general died, the sources he and Daniel had cultivated would hear the news and report to them at the rat-nest motel in Medellin. If Daniel made it out, he'd know to meet Alec there.

If Daniel made it out? Alec clenched his teeth and shoved the negativity aside. His partner *would* make it out of this hellhole and meet him in Medellin. Or, regardless of what they'd agreed, Alec *would* find his partner. No matter what it took.

Chapter 1

Alec stood in the motel bathroom, ready to chuck his cell phone into the toilet. The water would render the phone and all the data on it useless, erasing the last traces of his trail before he went underground. He'd been followed for a couple of days. The time had come for Alec Kincaid to disappear.

When he'd called the black ops team leader and told him he was going dark and extending his leave of absence indefinitely, he'd received an earful. Time for Alec to get his ass back on assignment, Briggs had bellowed. The team needed him.

Maybe so. But first Alec needed to lose his tail.

Though their orders came from unnamed officials within the U.S. government, the elite twelve-man team operated off the grid, an independent entity funded through offshore investments and hidden behind dummy corporations. Long before the Office of Homeland Security was formed, the team had been working for Uncle Sam in foreign hot spots or doing jobs the U.S. military couldn't legally tackle. The work was covert, dangerous…and lucrative.

At thirty-five, Alec could easily retire and live off his investments, so extending his personal leave time was not a hardship.

But, as Briggs had reminded him, the team was already short one man due to Daniel's disappearance. The team had changed Daniel's status from *MIA* to *presumed dead* after five months and given up their search.

Daniel. The only person he'd allowed himself to trust or give a damn about since his mother taught him his first hard lesson in misplaced loyalty, the pain of betrayal. Then Alec had abandoned his only friend. Maybe he was more like his mom than he wanted to believe. Didn't matter that he'd personally looked for Daniel for nine months. He'd gotten nowhere. He had no more information now about his partner's disappearance than he'd had that hellish afternoon in the Colombian jungle.

Alec swallowed the bile and sour guilt that swelled in his throat. As he held the phone out over the toilet, the screen lit up like the Christmas trees currently lining the streets of Denver. He paused, considered ignoring the ring. But Alec pulled the phone back and flipped it over. Just in case the call was Daniel, finally surfacing.

Checking the caller I.D., Alec recognized the name of the woman who'd bought his house in Cherry Creek last week. He frowned. Why the hell was she calling?

He conjured a mental image of the woman, and a kick of libido replaced his suspicion. Alec never forgot a face, especially one as stunning as Erin Bauer's. He'd ogled more than her face last week as he'd toted cardboard boxes out, and she'd carried wicker baskets and flowery pillows into his old house.

He started to toss the phone without answering, but a prick of unease stopped him. Not answering felt too much like leaving a loose end unresolved. Better to see what she wanted. "H'lo?"

"Um…Mr. Kincaid?" her sweet female voice chirped. "This is Erin Bauer. I bought your house on Hurley Street."

"Yeah?"

"Well, you have some mail here, and I was hoping you'd give me your forwarding address."

"Don't have one."

"Oh. Then…maybe you could stop by and pick it up? Although a lot of it's probably junk, there's a bill from the power company and a personal letter that looks impor—"

"Toss it all," he interrupted. He also remembered the woman's tendency to chatter nonstop.

"But—"

"I don't need it."

"Even the letter?" She sounded appalled. "It was hand-delivered by messenger this afternoon. It looks important."

"Hand-delivered?" Suspicion reared its head again. "Who's it from?"

In his line of work letters could be deadly. A piece of Detasheet fit easily inside an envelope to make a letter bomb. He preferred to deal by phone. By encrypted email.

"There's no return address," Erin said. "I could open it and read it to you if—"

"No!" A cold sweat popped out on his lip thinking of Erin's lush little body, blown to bits by an incendiary device intended for him.

She snorted indignantly. "Ooo-kay. Just an idea."

He'd have to go to the house and pick up the damn letter, if only to be sure she didn't snoop and get toasted in the process.

"There's a name or something in a corner on the back," she said.

His old house was almost certainly being watched. He couldn't just waltz up to the door without being seen. Alec rubbed the back of his neck and stewed over this hitch in his plans. Delays didn't sit well with him.

"It's hard to read the writing, but it looks like La-something." Erin paused. "Lafire, maybe?"

Alec jolted. "What?"

"The word in the corner of the envelope. It's written in chicken scratch, but it looks like Lafire or—"

A chill skittered down his neck. "Lafitte?"

"Uh, yeah. Maybe."

Alec's stomach somersaulted. His mind leapfrogged as he strode toward the motel door. "Listen carefully, Erin. Put the letter down." He kept his voice under tight control, even as adrenaline and hope surged through him. "Don't touch it again. Got it?"

He prayed she hadn't already obliterated any fingerprints on the envelope, destroyed evidence that could help him find Daniel.

"Uh, yeah. I got it." Her tone was rife with unspoken questions.

He expelled a harsh breath. "Look, I'll be there as soon as I can. In the meantime—"

He jammed on his shades and scanned the parking lot before stepping out into the December sunshine. Alec jerked open the driver's door of his rental car and dropped onto the front seat. Was the letter really from Daniel? And if it was, why hadn't Daniel come in person? Or sent an encrypted email? A letter was *not* protocol. Yet this letter could answer all his questions about what had happened to Daniel that fateful day months ago.

Or it could be a trap.

"In the meantime, what?" Erin asked.

Alec squeezed the phone. "Just sit tight. I'm on my way."

As he sped out of the parking lot, Alec pitched the cell phone in the motel swimming pool.

* * *

Lifting her face to the sun, Erin Bauer savored the unseasonably warm day before she stooped to collect her newspaper from the end of her driveway. By tomorrow, the weatherman said, conditions more typical of the Christmas season in Colorado would blast into town.

As she unfolded the newspaper, Erin scanned Hurley Street for signs of Alec Kincaid. More than two hours had passed since he'd said he was on his way. Not that she was watching the clock.

She skimmed the front page and gave the headlines a cursory glance. The top story remained the U.S. senator's daughter who'd disappeared from the charity medical delegation in Colombia. The senator was pleading for information about his only child's disappearance. Erin rubbed a hand over her abdomen. Her loose peasant shirt hid the fact that she could no longer button even her "fat jeans," though she was still a long way from needing maternity clothes. Tucking the newspaper under her arm, she sighed her sympathy for the senator whose daughter was missing. Erin understood loss.

Shoving down a twinge of loneliness, she swiped an errant curl of light brown hair from her eyes. Turning to go inside, she cast another expectant glance down the street. Okay, maybe she was looking forward to seeing Alec a little bit. After all, God didn't give many men the drool-worthy physique He'd gifted Alec with. Or eyes blue enough to send quivers to her core. So who could blame her for wanting another chance to goggle at the man?

Considering Alec had ignored her attempts to make friendly conversation, she'd had little else to do *but* admire his good looks as they moved their belongings last week.

If he weren't so…well, *unapproachable*…she'd consider inviting him to dinner or asking if he'd meet her for lunch one day. If she was truly making a fresh start in her life, she should think about dating again. It *had* been two years...

But the timing is all wrong now. Maybe next year...

A sharp pang twisted through her chest, and she sighed. She had to stop dwelling on Bradley's death, on the Finley child. She needed to push the horrid memories aside and move forward.

Pivoting on her toe, she headed inside to unpack another box in her study. One thing was certain—the next man she let into her life had to be the safe, reliable, homebody sort. No more following her man off the edge of mountains, jumping from planes or diving in treacherous waters. She had other people to think about, other lives to consider, responsibilities. *She had guilt.*

Erin puffed stray hair out of her face and pushed the gloomy thoughts aside. She set out the few Christmas decorations she owned—a jolly Santa, her mother's nativity set and a pine garland, which gave her new mantel a touch of holiday cheer. For the next half hour, she immersed herself in unpacking her collection of books. Beloved original copies of Faulkner, Caldwell and Steinbeck, passed down from her father, graced the shelves next to signed copies of her favorite romance novels and mysteries. Textbooks on topics as varied as meteorology and art history testified to her thirst for knowledge, inherited from her mother and the reason she'd become a teacher. Again pain filtered through her chest. She *would* teach again. But she'd be more careful this time. *Much* more careful.

She heard a car in her driveway and moved to the window to peer outside, hoping Alec had finally arrived. Instead she found a delivery van from a local florist pulling to a stop by her sidewalk.

Erin hurried to the front door in time to see a man dressed in a Santa suit slide out of the van. Not Alec. Disappointment spiraled through her, followed closely by curiosity. Who could be sending her flowers? He had to have the wrong address.

She grinned, remembering the silly ads she'd seen for the innovative florist, touting their army of Santas on staff to make special deliveries more festive. The Santas would even sing for an extra fee. The Santa in her driveway unloaded a large poinsettia, tugged his fur-trimmed hat lower over his ears and marched up the walk to her porch.

She stepped out on her porch and called a greeting to the elderly gentleman. He gave her a small nod of acknowledgment. Erin couldn't hide the note of amusement in her voice when she asked, "Hello, Santa. Are you sure those are for me?"

"Yes, ma'am." He lumbered awkwardly in his overstuffed costume up her porch stairs and raised his head. The piercing blue eyes that greeted Erin and her answering bone-deep tremor sent a crackling jolt of awareness through her.

"And you have a letter of mine," Alec said.

She gasped her surprise. Even at close range, the white beard and chubby cheeks looked real. "Mr. Kincaid?"

Alec held a hand up and shook his head slightly. "Inside."

"After you." She stepped back and waved him inside. "So, moonlighting as an elf?"

His expression was hard and unamused. Erin's grin faltered. She had known Alec was remote, but his lack of humor was unsettling. Once inside, Alec placed the poinsettia on her end table and fiddled a bit with the bow before turning.

Erin waved a hand toward her unpacked boxes. "Sorry it's such a mess. I haven't finished in here. I thought the kitchen was—"

Alec turned his back to her and walked down the hall, opening closet doors and casting a sweeping gaze into each room. She followed him, bristling at his rudeness. He may have lived here once, but this was *her* home now.

"Looking for something, Santa?" She didn't bother to hide the irritation in her voice. "I have your letter out here—" she hitched a thumb over her shoulder "—if that's what—"

He closed the blinds in her bedroom before he faced her. "Have you noticed anyone hanging around the area? Any weird phone calls or strangers come by here?"

This from a man wearing red velvet pants and a fake white beard?

Erin couldn't resist. "You mean stranger than you?"

He scowled and moved toward her. "Just answer the question. Have you seen anyone watching the house?"

A tingle of alarm skipped down her back. "No. Should I have?"

"Not necessarily." He peeled off the faux beard, which he'd apparently applied with some sticky gluelike substance, and rubbed the black stubble on his square jaw. "Can I see the letter now?"

Erin stared at him, puzzling over his peculiar demeanor before backing toward the hall. "Sure. In here."

She led him to the living room and collected his letter from the coffee table. When she thrust it toward him, he hissed and winced.

"I asked you not to touch it again," he grated through his teeth. He took the letter from her carefully, holding it by the edges.

She gave her head a little shake and drew a slow breath. "Sorry."

He grunted and bent his head to study the envelope.

Just humor him a little longer. Erin shifted her weight and rubbed her palms on the seat of her jeans. "So…you recognize the handwriting or anything?"

He didn't answer at first, but when he raised his gaze, she'd swear she saw a flicker of emotion in his eyes. Her pulse stumbled.

"Never mind that," he said huskily. "Don't tell anyone I was here or say anything about having seen the letter. Understand?" A muscle in his rugged jaw twitched.

"Well...yeah. But why?"

His stern demeanor had returned so quickly, she wondered if she'd really seen the flash of pain and vulnerability she'd imagined.

"Just keep quiet about it. Do you have a zip-seal bag I can put this in?"

"A bag?"

"To preserve it."

"In the kitchen. I'll be right back." Erin hustled past Alec, bemused by his dictate of silence.

When she returned with a zip-sealing sandwich bag, Alec gently slid the letter into it and tucked it inside the fuzzy lapel of the Santa suit. Immediately he headed for the door with a long-legged stride. "Remember, you never saw this letter. Keep your doors locked, and if you think you're being followed, don't take any chances. Go to the cops. Got it?"

Erin's pulse did a little two-step in her chest. "Alec, is there a reason you think I might be followed or in danger? If so, I think I have a right to know what—"

"No." Alec grimaced and sighed heavily. "I...just think women like you, who live alone, should...be careful." He quirked his mouth up in a lopsided grin that looked more like a wince. "Merry Christmas." Quickly he replaced the fake beard and shouldered through the front door, changing his gait as he stepped out on the porch to an old man's shuffle.

"Thanks for the poinsettia, Al—uh, Santa." Rolling her eyes, Erin closed the front door. "Weird."

Maybe she was better off not dating if Alec was the sort of fruitcake that the bachelor world had to offer.

Her stomach rumbled. *Mmm, fruitcake.*

She glanced at her watch and decided to have a snack before doing any more unpacking. On her way into the kitchen, Erin stuck her finger in the soil around the poinsettia. Bone dry. Carrying the plant to the kitchen sink, she gave it a drink from the spray nozzle. While that water soaked in, she opened a cabinet and took down a glass.

A floorboard behind her creaked, her only warning before a powerful hand was clapped over her mouth. She loosed a muffled scream, and the glass fell to the floor, shattering.

"Shut up, and do what I say!" a low voice hissed. The hand over her mouth was removed, and a cool knife blade pressed against her throat. In the tinted glass of the microwave, Erin caught a reflection of the paunchy man behind her.

Her knees trembled, but she fought not to let them buckle. Not with the thug's knife squeezing her jugular.

Focus. Don't let fear win, she heard Bradley saying as clearly as if he were still around, goading her into doing another daring stunt. She remembered steeling her nerves to launch her hang glider on her first trip with Bradley, calming her jitters in order to think clearly the first time she parachuted solo. She had to muster the same clearheaded thinking now, despite her fear.

"Where's LeCroix's letter?" the man growled.

Her stomach churned as she recalled Alec's warning. He'd known she would be in danger, yet he'd given her nothing but a warning to deny seeing his letter. Damn him!

"Wh-what letter?"

Her captor shook her, and the blade nicked her neck. His grip around her waist tightened.

Erin gasped and slid a protective hand to her lower abdomen.

A second man appeared from behind her and began ransacking her kitchen drawers.

"Come on, sweetheart. I know you called Kincaid. Now where's Daniel LeCroix's letter?"

"I don't know anything about a letter. Please let me go!"

"Lady, either you talk now, or I'll cut you until you tell us what we want. Where is the letter that was delivered here this afternoon?"

Erin whimpered as the knife pressed harder against her neck. She was out of her league here, as well as outnumbered. Her captor knew she was lying, had clearly tapped her phone, probably had been watching her house. Alec had suspected as much, ergo the disguise and the drawn blinds.

Whatever Alec was involved in, she wanted nothing to do with it or the seedy men who were after him. Despite Alec's warning, she refused to anger these men by lying. She wouldn't risk her life for something she knew nothing about.

"I don't have the letter. Not anymore."

Even as Alec adjusted the tiny listening device in his ear, he heard the growling threats against Erin, heard her give him up.

Damn. They'd been closer behind him than he'd thought.

"I swear. The letter isn't here anymore," Erin said, the fear in her voice coming clearly through the microphone hidden in the poinsettia. Alec thought of the shadows that had clouded Erin's wide dark eyes as he'd left. The doubts. *The vulnerability.*

He cursed the twist of fate that had put Erin in the line of fire.

"Where is it?" the male voice growled.

"Alec has it. He just left. In a florist's van."

So much for denials. Alec finished stripping off the bulky Santa suit and fled the delivery van Erin had just identified. Checking the chamber of his SIG-Sauer pistol, Alec crept from behind the van to the cover of a large holly bush.

Don't jeopardize the mission. If things go south, it's every man for himself.

The principle wasn't complicated. Easy enough to understand. Just not so easy to follow through on. Not when the man involved is your partner, your best friend.

Or an innocent woman with wounded, puppy-dog brown eyes.

Alec bit out an expletive. He couldn't abandon Erin to the thugs who had her. Not when he was the one they wanted. Him—and Daniel's letter. Though he knew civilian casualties were sometimes unavoidable in counterterrorism, he wasn't ready to write Erin Bauer off as a cost of war just yet.

Having parked the van out of sight a few blocks from Erin's house, he now ran through his former neighbors' backyards, listening closely to the exchange playing from his earphone as he circled back to Erin's house.

"How long ago did Kincaid leave?"

"Just a few minutes."

With a running leap, Alec hurtled the picket fence at 217 Hurley Street, dodged the garbage cans at 215 and raced through the lines of drying laundry behind 213.

"Did he read the letter before he left?"

"No."

"Who delivered it? What did it say?"

Jumping the hedge between 211 and 209, he sprinted to the backyard of Erin's next-door neighbor. From behind a giant shrub, he surveyed the scene at his old house.

"I don't know. I s-swear. I d-don't know anything."

"We'll see about that."

He heard Erin yelp. In pain or fear? Adrenaline kicked in his chest. Needing to get a better fix on the situation, he calculated his best approach.

"Come on, sweetheart. You're coming with us."

What?

"What?" Erin's terrified voice echoed Alec's reaction. He pressed a hand to his ear, holding the tiny receiver closer.

"Kincaid couldn't have gotten far. We'll take you with us as a bargaining chip, offer you as trade. His girlfriend for the letter."

Girlfriend? Alec cursed again under his breath. If they thought Erin meant something to him, her life was in even more danger.

"But I'm not—"

"Shut up, lady. Move it."

"No, wait! I—"

Alec heard an *oof,* a grunt. The scuffle of feet. A crash.

From his hiding place at the side of the house, he heard the back door open. Muffled voices. He peered around the corner and saw them drag Erin at knifepoint toward a white SUV. The hair at Alec's nape bristled. If they harmed so much as a hair on Erin's head...

Guilt wrenched inside him. This was his fault. She was at risk because of him. Obviously, the thugs planned to use her as bait to draw him out. Therefore, freeing her, protecting her was his duty, his obligation.

Another man had joined the knife-wielding cretin and climbed behind the steering wheel. Alec didn't recognize either of the men, but he memorized their faces now. As the guy manhandling Erin shoved her in the back seat, he snarled some kind of warning. Despite her obvious fear, Erin lifted her chin defiantly.

Alec's lips twitched at her show of moxie. He'd found no shortage of things to admire about Erin Bauer. He couldn't blame her for giving up the information about the letter so easily. She had no way to know what was at stake, no reason to do as he'd directed. Even he didn't know what was at play or why. But now Erin was a part of it...which left him rescuing her. The old-fashioned way. The hard way.

He gritted his teeth, irritated by the diversion from his plans. He'd finally picked up Daniel's trail. He needed to be studying the message his partner had sent, going underground, lying low until he lost the tail he'd picked up. But he wouldn't, *couldn't* abandon Erin to these men.

Like you abandoned Daniel.

The white SUV turned down Hurley Street, and Alec retraced his path, running through the neighbors' yards, keeping the vehicle in sight. He kept pace with the SUV until it turned onto the main street leading to the interstate.

Time for wheels.

A pickup truck stopped at the intersection, and Alec snatched open the door. "Police! Follow that white SUV. Don't lose them!"

The college-aged driver scowled his doubt. "Let's see some I.D., bud."

Alec pulled his SIG-Sauer from his shoulder holster. "Move it!"

The young man paled and raised his palms. "Easy, bro. I'm going!"

Alec pointed. "There! They just got on the interstate. Hurry!"

His driver punched the gas, wove through traffic like an expert, and merged onto the interstate doing close to eighty.

Alec spotted the SUV several cars ahead and calculated his best attack. He didn't want Erin's captors to see him and risk a car chase that put innocent lives at risk. An eighteen-wheeler occupied the next lane, and Alec sized up his options. Doable.

"Pull as close to the back of that truck as you can and hold it steady. Got it?"

The college kid looked at him and nodded. "Check."

While his chauffeur aligned his pickup with the larger truck, Alec rolled down the passenger window and secured his SIG-Sauer in his holster.

"Thanks for the lift," Alec said as he wedged his body

through the window and hoisted himself out. While they rocketed down the interstate, Alec climbed into the pickup's bed. Braced against the air current. Focused on his task, his mission.

The pickup moved beside the rear of the eighteen-wheeler, and Alec eyed the bar ladder on the back end of the truck. He prepared. Calculated. Jumped.

His foot slipped as the truck bounced over a pothole. Adrenaline spiking, he groped for a rung of the bar-ladder. The jolt as he caught himself tugged viciously on his shoulder. Pain slithered down his arm, but he held on, found a foothold.

Over the whoosh of air and rumble of engines, he heard the pickup's driver whoop. He nodded to the young man as the pickup eased back into the correct lane.

"Kids, don't try this at home." Alec scaled the rungs on the back of the eighteen-wheeler and levered himself to the roof. The truck rocked and shimmied as it barreled down the road. The slipstream pushed and pulled at him as Alec found his footing. Like surfing in a hurricane.

Keeping his center of balance low, he edged along the roof of the truck's trailer. Scanning the road in front of him, he spotted the SUV. The luggage rack on its roof. Target located.

The eighteen-wheeler changed lanes, easing forward. *That's it. A little further.*

A passing car honked, and a passenger gestured wildly at the driver of the eighteen-wheeler.

Alec gritted his teeth. Damn it, he didn't want attention drawn to him! But, realistically, he had to accept that his highway gymnastics would cause spectator concern. The sooner he acted, the better.

Alec edged into position. The SUV was still almost a car length away, but he couldn't wait much longer, couldn't risk

Erin's captors seeing him. He braced himself and judged the distance to the roof of the SUV.

A challenge. But doable.

What could she do? Erin squeezed the door handle and weighed her options. Jumping out of the car at highway speed would be suicide. But when they left the interstate, if they stopped for a traffic light…

She rubbed her palm on the leg of her jeans, over her belly. She had to be careful. Couldn't take unnecessary risks.

But she refused to let these men harm her, kidnap her without even a token resistance. She wouldn't go down without a fight.

She thought of Alec Kincaid, the selfish bastard, walking out on her, leaving her to fend for her life. Alone. She was in this mess because of his stupid letter! She worked up a good mad and funneled the energy toward planning her escape. They had to get off the interstate sometime. And when they did…

A car behind them honked, and she absently turned her attention to the passenger-side mirror. An idea niggled. Maybe she could signal someone in another car….

She glanced sideways to the knife-wielding maniac who rode beside her and nixed that thought. She couldn't tip her hand. When she acted, she had to catch the men totally off guard.

She returned her gaze to the side mirror with a wistful glance. If only—

Erin sat straighter in the seat and narrowed her gazed in disbelief. A man was on top of the eighteen-wheeler behind them!

What kind of idiot—?

Her breath caught, and she blinked to make sure her eyes weren't playing tricks on her.

No trick. It was Alec.

Her heart, responding to Alec's daring with a drumroll, rose to her throat. She stifled the gasp that threatened, determined not to give Alec's presence away to Mr. Knife and his buddy. Her gaze riveted to the SUV's side mirror. Her fingernails cut into her palms.

Horrified, she watched Alec inch along the roof of the truck's trailer. He crouched low, adjusted his arms for balance.

Dear God! What was he planning?

An image of Bradley's broken body flashed in Erin's mind, and her stomach rolled. Alec was coming to help her. Like Bradley had been. Putting himself in danger. Risking his life. Taking foolish chances. For her.

The bitter taste of fear filled her mouth, and Erin swallowed a moan. *Not again.*

"You say something, sweetheart?"

Erin jerked her head around to face Knife. "N-no."

"Take it easy, darlin'," Knife said with a sadistic leer. "Soon as we get that letter back from Kincaid, you'll be free to go."

The man driving grunted. "For a swim with the fishies maybe."

Knife laughed and gave Erin a salacious wink. "Don't worry, sweetheart. I'll take care of ya."

A shudder raced down her spine. She worked to form enough spit to swallow the knot in her throat as she swung her gaze back to the mirror. The truck was closer. Alec perched on the edge of the trailer, crouching. Springing.

Erin gasped, but the sound was lost as Alec landed with a thump on the roof of the SUV.

"What the hell was that?" the driver barked.

Trembling all over, Erin held her breath.

Knife angled his head, looking up. "Something hit the roof."

Suddenly the window beside Knife shattered. Erin jolted as glass shards blasted across the seat.

"What the—!" The SUV swerved as the startled driver twisted toward the smashed window.

"It's Kincaid!" Knife brushed broken glass off his shirt and surged forward to shout to his cohort. "He's on the roof! Shake him!"

Erin gripped the edge of the seat as their driver snatched the steering wheel hard to the left then right again. Alec's legs slid off the passenger side of the roof, scrambling to find purchase.

Panic roiled inside her. "No!"

The driver yanked the steering wheel again. Alec slipped farther down the side of the SUV. He needed help. Her help.

Snatching off her seat belt, Erin lunged for the front seat, the driver, the steering wheel.

"Hey, get back here!" Knife grabbed the back of her shirt. She fought like a wildcat to grab the wheel, steady the SUV.

Erin heard a thump, a smack. When Knife's hold on her suddenly fell away, she darted a glance over her shoulder.

Alec hung over the other side of the car now. He reached in through the broken window to land a punch in Knife's jaw.

Knife's eyes rolled back. Before the man could even slump all the way to the seat, Alec slid, feet first, through the broken window.

"Manny?" the driver called as he checked the rearview mirror.

"Manny's taking a nap," her rescuer said.

"Alec!" Relief swamped her so hard and fast she nearly choked on the tears.

But her relief came too soon. The driver raised an arm, turned, and leveled a gun at her.

She saw the flash from the muzzle in the same instant the

ear-shattering blast rang in her ears. She screamed and curled forward to protect her abdomen.

More glass rained on her as the passenger-side window shattered.

"Get up!" Alec shouted.

She glanced up and realized the command was directed to her. He struggled to restrain the driver, keep the thug from shooting again and steer the SUV at the same time. She met Alec's blazing blue gaze, and instant admiration stole her breath.

He hitched his head toward the front seat. "Hurry! Grab the wheel!"

Erin scrambled to suit orders to action. Somehow Alec managed to hold the SUV in one lane. But as the thug struggled with Alec, the man's foot moved on and off the accelerator making the SUV jerk, lunge and stall. They drifted toward the next lane and swapped paint with a school bus. Alec cursed.

Heart thundering, Erin clambered into the front seat, wedged her left foot over to the accelerator pedal and wrapped her hands around the steering wheel.

Freed of needing to steady the vehicle, Alec squeezed the driver's throat, held him immobile until the man went limp.

Erin gawked and leaned out of the way as Alec dragged the man's body into the back seat. "Is he dead?"

"No. I want these jokers alive to answer questions."

Erin slid into the driver's seat and brought the SUV under control.

"You okay?" Alec asked.

"Depends. Define *okay*." She met his eyes in the rearview mirror. "If I were shaking any harder, my t-teeth would rattle, and I feel like I m-might throw up, but…I'm not hurt. Does that count?"

"Can you drive for a while?" His face was hard, his gaze razor sharp.

She nodded.

"Good enough for me." He situated the thugs on the back seat, tying their hands with the seat belt. "Take the next exit, but don't stop. Drive until you find a place that has some privacy."

"O-okay." Erin flipped on her turn signal and changed lanes, heading for the exit he indicated.

Alec climbed into the front seat beside her and raised his shirt to pull out the envelope tucked in the waist of his jeans. He heaved a relieved-sounding sigh and closed his eyes.

Crisis averted. Thanks to Alec's heroics. Erin exhaled her own relieved sigh, but her hands still trembled. She cast a sideways glance at Alec, and for a moment, she simply savored the sight of his black, windblown hair, the stark bone structure of his brow and jaw, the full cut of his mouth.

When they'd been hauling boxes last week, she'd been transfixed by his taut, muscular frame, by his intensely blue eyes. But it seemed this man's face was perhaps the most striking, the most interesting of his features. Without being classically handsome, he had a rugged sort of appeal. A muscle in his jaw jumped as he clenched his teeth and opened his eyes. She followed his lowered gaze to the envelope in his lap.

She scowled. "That dumb letter must be awfully important."

He cut her a sideways glance. "It is to me."

Harsh lines bracketed his mouth, his eyes, and spoke of hard living. A thin, pale scar on his cheek evidenced a past injury. Alec Kincaid was clearly no stranger to a dangerous lifestyle.

Her annoyance cooled when she realized the lengths to which he'd gone to rescue her. He was either the craziest man on the planet or the bravest. She'd wager on the latter.

"Thank you," she murmured. "For helping me. Saving me."

He didn't answer. Instead he turned to stare out the side window, his face an emotionless mask. Finally he slanted a hooded look at her and grunted. "Your gratitude may be premature."

Chapter 2

Following Alec's directions, Erin pulled the SUV behind a self-storage building and cut the engine. She cast him a wary gaze across the front seat. "Now what?"

Alec scanned the area with predatory eyes. "I'm going to have a little talk with these cretins. I need to find out who they are and who sent them."

"Shouldn't we call the police?" Still shivering from cold and fear, Erin chafed her arms. The action drew Alec's attention and a dark frown.

"No police."

"What?" Erin blinked her shock. "They broke into my house, held me at knifepoint, kidnapped me, threatened to kill me.... You better believe I'm calling the cops!"

His expression grew flinty. "*No.* I'll handle this."

"Why? Are you FBI or something?"

"Or something." Alec climbed out of the SUV and opened the back door. He checked the two unconscious men, then used the knife the first man had held at her throat to slice through the seat belt. With amazing ease and his impressive muscles taut, Alec hoisted the unconscious driver over his shoulder and carried him to the side of the self-storage building.

A funny catch lodged in Erin's chest as she watched Alec pat the thug down, ostensibly checking for other weapons, then return to the SUV. He'd saved her life. For that, she figured she owed him the benefit of the doubt, even if the notion of not reporting this terrifying incident to the police galled her. She glanced at the letter sitting on the console between the front seats. What was so darned important about that letter that men were willing to kill for it?

Alec ducked his head in the back seat again and sawed on the strap securing the second man.

"So what am I supposed to do?" she asked. "Just go back home and pretend nothing happened?"

Alec's hands stilled, and he glanced up at her, his mouth set in a grim line.

Erin wondered if Alec ever smiled, wondered about the life he led that kept his expression so hard and humorless. Wondered how a smile would transform his stony features.

"Once I get this guy out, I want you to dump this vehicle somewhere, then walk about a mile before you call a cab. Don't go back to your house. They know you live there, and you'd be an easy mark."

Erin pressed a hand to her stomach as anxiety fueled the wave of nausea that swamped her. "And why would they come back for me? I thought it was you and this Daniel LeCroix person's letter that they were after."

He sighed, and the muscles in his jaw jumped. "Because I made a mistake."

"A mistake?"

He grunted and continued his work. "I came back for you. Rescued you from them."

She scoffed. "You see that as a mistake?"

"Now they believe I care whether you live or die. They'll see you as a way to get to me."

Dread settled in her chest like a rock.

"Do you have a friend or relative you can stay with for a while?"

A hollow ache plucked at her. Loneliness. Grief. And guilt, her constant companion of late. "No. My parents are dead, and I just moved into town last week."

He scowled. "Then go to a hotel. And be careful. Keep your door locked and don't talk to anyone."

"But—" Before she had a chance to voice her complaint, the scuffle of feet drew Alec's attention to the side of the storage building. The SUV driver had regained consciousness. Hands still bound by the seat belt, the groggy man stumbled to his feet. And ran.

"Damn!" Alec snatched his gun from his waistband and foisted it toward her. "Watch this guy. If he so much as blinks, shoot him!"

Spinning away, Alec sprinted after the fleeing driver. Erin gaped at Alec's retreating back then down at the weapon he'd shoved in her hands. *Shoot Mr. Knife?* Even if her own life were at stake, she wasn't sure she could ever pull the trigger, kill another human being.

Her stomach swirled, and she wished she had some crackers to settle the queasiness. She'd moved to Colorado hoping to build a new life, to escape the turmoil and tragedy that had plagued her the past two years. To heal, to make a fresh start, and to nurture Bradley's last gift to her. But she'd only been in her new home a week, and already bad luck and danger had found her again. She had to be jinxed.

Hands shaking, she set the gun on the passenger's seat, terrified her trembling hands would make the gun fire accidentally.

Her gaze darted to the letter—the root of this whole fiasco, the source of the danger she was in. She lifted the missive and held it to the sunlight, trying to see what was inside. Useless. The envelope paper was too thick.

It occurred to her that, like the driver, Knife could rouse, could surprise her, could overpower her. Could steal the letter and escape.

Then all of Alec's efforts to hold on to the letter and rescue her would have been in vain. Mind spinning, Erin turned the letter over in her hand. Maybe she couldn't bring herself to shoot Knife if needed, but she could do something to protect Daniel's letter.

Grumbling to himself in disgust, Alec balled his hands as he stormed back to the storage units where he'd left Erin. He'd lost his prey in the maze of alleys, small homes and parked cars. Worse than that, he'd taken off after the cretin so fast, he'd left Daniel's letter sitting on the front console of the SUV. While mapping out a plan to keep Erin safe, he'd allowed her fearful eyes, her rebellious pout to distract him. For a man who prided himself on perfection, today's accumulating list of mistakes chafed.

He sidled up to the back wall of the storage building and peered around the corner to survey the scene at the SUV. If Erin had lost control of the situation, he didn't want to walk into a confrontation unaware.

Erin paced back and forth behind the rear bumper. Her attention remained glued down the driveway, in the direction he'd pursued the driver. As she marched back and forth, she gnawed a thumbnail, then frowned at the chewed finger. A bulge at the small of her back told him where she'd stashed his SIG-Sauer.

He didn't see the other thug, but that could mean the man was still slumped in the back seat.

A shadow shifted near the front fender, and Alec tensed.

He pulled out the knife he'd been using to cut the seat belts and narrowed his gaze. Grass rustled by the driver's-side tire.

Alec moved out, skulking toward the SUV with the knife ready. He'd only made it a few steps before cretin number two sprang from behind the vehicle.

The bastard lofted a thick branch and closed in on Erin.

"Erin, look out!" Alec shouted.

Too late. The heavy branch crashed down on her skull, and she crumpled to the ground. Alec's gut lurched with a sickening dread.

As her assailant bolted down the driveway, he snatched something from the front pocket of her jeans. An envelope.

Alec cursed. Racing to Erin, he fished the SIG-Sauer out from under her shirt and darted down the drive after the escaping thief. He fired a shot as the man dashed around the corner of a clapboard house. Training told Alec to go after the fleeing suspect, but the woman lying, unmoving, in the dirt spoke to something deeper in Alec's soul.

You left Daniel.

He stared at the spot where Erin's assailant had disappeared another moment, a razor pain slicing through him when he thought of the lost letter, the danger Daniel could be in with his missive in the wrong hands.

Yet seeing Daniel's handwriting had fired new hope in him that his partner was alive. Guilt and regret fueled his determination to get his search back on track.

As soon as he was certain Erin was safe.

He'd be damned if he knew why this woman compelled him to break with procedure, to jeopardize his mission, to act counter to everything he'd been trained to do. The inconsistency needled him.

Rushing back down the driveway, he dropped to his knees beside the unconscious woman and felt for a pulse. He released a deep breath when he found a strong throbbing beat in her neck.

Pulling her into his lap, he carefully examined her head for the goose egg sure to be swelling on her scalp. Her feminine scent teased him, and her silky curls coiled seductively around his fingers. Her limp body, her slack face, her vulnerability speared to his core. He'd been trained to steel himself against softer emotions, sympathies that could jeopardize a mission and blur his professional focus. But something about this woman slipped under his defenses and burrowed deep inside him.

Wincing, Erin jerked and raised a hand to the spot on her head where he probed. "Ow."

Her eyelids fluttered open. With a gasp, she tried to sit up, but he caught her shoulders and eased her back to his lap. "Easy. You took a nasty blow. Go slow."

Her puppy-dog eyes turned up to his face. "Alec?"

So she could talk and her short-term memory was intact. Both good signs. He focused on her pupils rather than the sexy sweetness of her mahogany eyes. Even. No abnormal dilation.

"Are you dizzy? Numb anywhere?" he asked.

She squeezed her eyes shut and rubbed her head. "I… No. My head hurts like fire, though. What happened?"

"Your charge cracked a limb over your head." He was prepared to chastise her for her inattention to her prisoner, but she moaned in misery as she sat up.

"Knife! Where'd he—" She whipped her head around, apparently looking for the thug, then yelped and cradled her head again.

"I said go slow." He slid a hand under her elbow to steady her. "And your man got away after he whacked you."

"Sorry." She grimaced, and her face paled as she clapped a hand to her jeans pocket. "It's gone. The envelope—"

Alec gritted his teeth as renewed frustration wrenched inside him. "He took it."

Next, Erin patted her chest, and a corner of her mouth curled up. When she unfastened the top button of her shirt and jammed her hand inside her bra, Alec arched an eyebrow, undeniably intrigued. A flash of heat spun through his blood as his attention was drawn to the curve of breast that peeked from her open neckline.

Erin chuckled and drew something out of her clothes. A folded paper.

He sent her a dubious frown. "What's that?"

Her answering smile beamed, its wattage hitting him like a punch in the solar plexus. "Your letter."

Alec stilled. "What?"

She extended the folded sheet to him, smug satisfaction glowing in her eyes. "I figured Knife might try to steal the letter again, so I hid the contents of the envelope. Just in case. I put the envelope in my pocket, so it'd look like I was at least trying to protect it. I figured if I left it completely unguarded Knife might get suspicious. I made the slit in the side as small and inconspicuous as I could."

As Erin prattled on, explaining her reasoning, Alec slipped the letter from her fingers and heaved a mental sigh of relief. Amazing. Erin's forethought and creativity, the fact that she'd bothered at all to protect Daniel's letter, stunned him. Impressed the hell out of him.

When she stopped chattering about her ingenuity, she met his gaze with an expectant expression. "Pretty good, huh?"

"Smart thinking. I could kiss you."

She sent him a startled look, and he realized belatedly what he'd said.

When her gaze shifted to his mouth, adrenaline kicked his pulse up a notch. As if he'd just spotted a tango in the jungle. As if he'd just blown a hole in a building with a chunk of C4. As if…he had the opportunity to taste the lips of a gorgeous woman.

He dropped his gaze to her mouth, and the air around him charged with a crackling energy. Acting purely on impulse, Alec leaned toward Erin, zeroing in on his target. But before he reached his goal, Erin drew a sharp breath, moaned softly and clutched her gut. "Oh, geez. I—I think I'm gonna be sick."

Pinching the bridge of his nose, Alec shook off the fog that had momentarily muddled his mind. Another lapse in his thinking, another failure to let his training guide his actions.

He clenched his teeth, shoved to his feet and turned his attention back to the pale-faced woman who held her stomach. "What kind of pain are you having? Any dizziness or ringing ears?"

She flashed a chagrined smile. "Nausea. Sorry, this won't be pretty."

With that, she rolled to her hands and knees and retched. Not good. Vomiting was indication she could have a concussion. He crouched beside her and helped her trap her long hair inside the collar of her shirt. A loose curl escaped, and he held it away from her face as she heaved again. "You need to see a doctor."

She shook her head and several hanks of hair fell loose again. "I'll be fine."

"Don't be stupid."

Like he had room to talk. He'd almost kissed her. *Stupid, stupid…*

Slipups like that in the field could get you killed. Falling for a pair of seductive brown eyes or the temptation of a kiss was just the kind of mistake his enemies banked on. If he was going to find Daniel, he had to pull himself together.

Erin glared at him over her shoulder.

He gentled his voice. "You've had a serious head trauma,

and you're throwing up. You could have a concussion. You need a CT scan." He gathered her loose hair again and re-tucked it in her shirt, painfully aware of the silky texture against his skin.

She rocked back on her heels and swiped her mouth with her sleeve. "All I need is some crackers or something to settle my stomach. I'll be fine."

He narrowed his eyes and set his jaw. He didn't have time to argue with her. "You're going to see a doctor."

Erin twisted her lips in a frown of disagreement. Pushing to her feet, she dusted the seat of her jeans and, with a wobble, stepped toward the SUV. "Just take me home. Please?"

He shadowed her, ready to catch the stubborn woman if she toppled over. "I already told you why you can't go back to your house. Especially now with your buddy Knife, as you called him, and his cohort on the loose again."

"You really think they'll come after me again?" She furrowed her brow and held a hand to the knot rising on her scalp.

An external knot. A good sign.

"You really think they'll give up?" he returned.

Fear flickered across her face, and her shoulders drooped. "Great."

Alec calculated which emergency room was closest and internally groaned at the three- to four-hour wait they'd likely have on a Saturday afternoon. He toyed with, then nixed, the idea of leaving Erin at the hospital. She was in no condition to take care of herself. *Hell.*

More delays. More time for the people on his trail to track him. More opportunity for Erin to be found, caught, used against him, perhaps killed when Knife figured out she'd duped him and he didn't have Daniel's letter. He'd have to stay with her. Rather, she'd have to stay with him....

His gut tightened at the thought. Could he risk taking her

with him to the safe house in the mountains? And did he really have any other options if he was going to keep her safe?

Maybe if she weren't in danger because of him, he could justify leaving her at the E.R. The staff at the hospital would take care of her injuries. But the staff couldn't guard her from knife-wielding thugs the way he could. And Alec was certain the men who'd kidnapped her to force his hand would try again.

"Look, I appreciate your concern, Alec." Erin's face had more color, but she still visibly trembled. "But my head already feels better. It's only a sharp throb now." She tossed him a wry grin. "And I'm only sick to my stomach because I'm—" Her eyes slid closed, and she staggered. "Whoa, why is the ground moving?"

Alec caught her as she toppled. "That settles it, sweetcakes. You're coming with me."

"I don't—"

"Stop arguing and get in the truck."

While he helped her to the front seat of the SUV, Alec mentally ran down his list of contacts in the area, wishing he hadn't tossed his cell phone quite so soon. He stopped at a small insurance office, parking the damaged SUV out of sight, and convinced the receptionist to let him borrow the office phone and call in a few favors.

Within minutes he was escorting Erin into a private, outpatient radiology lab. The facility's owner was the brother of a former black ops teammate Alec had once rescued from a Honduran prison. Though the private lab was typically closed on Saturdays, the owner/radiologist met Alec to repay his brother's debt. While Erin was in the back getting her scan, Alec took a seat in the waiting area and recalculated his plans, adding Erin into the mix. Inconvenient, but doable.

He pulled Daniel's letter out and stared at the folded sheet. Erin had been lucky as hell the letter hadn't been a bomb.

He'd been waiting until he could dust the envelope for fingerprints, x-ray it and check for explosives before he opened the letter. Now there seemed no reason not to take his first close look at his only clue to Daniel's whereabouts.

Carefully, Alec unfolded the stiff paper. Colorful artwork and old-fashioned script decorated the page. Dotted lines connected one small drawing to another, superimposed on a map of a fictional Caribbean isle. In the top corner, the skull and crossbones of a pirate's flag smirked at Alec.

He frowned. Why would Daniel send him this child's souvenir? Was his partner simply telling him he was alive or did the map mean something else?

"Good news."

Drawn from his perusal of the pirate map by the radiologist's voice, Alec hastily refolded the sheet and shoved it in his pocket.

"Your friend has only a minor concussion," the radiologist said with a grin. "Chances are she'll have a whopping headache for a few days, but I see no other damage, nothing that concerns me. She should be just fine."

Alec nodded. "Can she travel?"

"Some, but she'll need lots of rest. Keep tabs on her, especially for the next twenty-four to thirty-six hours. Watch her pupils, her pulse rate. And wake her every couple hours and ask her basic questions about her name and the date. If her condition goes south, get her to a hospital immediately."

A technician escorted Erin into the waiting room, and Erin glared at Alec. "If you have any humanity at all, you will stop at the first hamburger joint we see and buy me a large cheeseburger with fries. I was hungry before. Now I'm famished."

Hypoglycemia, Alec thought, sizing up Erin's glower. *That'd explain her crankiness, too.*

He drove them to a fast-food restaurant drive-through where he ordered himself a double hamburger, then watched in amazement as Erin put away her dinner in record time. After devouring her meal, she settled back in the seat with a satisfied sigh.

"If you're sure I can't go home…" Erin yawned. "Then drop me at a hotel. This has been a heck of a day, and I'm bushed." Her eyelids drooped, and she nestled her cheek against the shoulder strap of the seat belt.

"Don't worry," Alec said. "I'm taking you someplace safe."

Erin woke to a loud droning sound and a throbbing ache at her temple. The pounding headache she understood—Knife had clobbered her when he escaped. The noisy rumble confused her, concerned her.

She cracked open her eyes and surveyed the dim, confined space where she lay. This wasn't the SUV. "Alec?"

"You're awake. Good."

She angled her head toward his voice and found him peering over his shoulder from a narrow seat at the front of the confined space. He wore a headset over one ear with a microphone at his mouth. The green glow of a control panel cast harsh shadows on his angular face and square jaw. "I was just about to wake you. Can you tell me who the president is?"

She did. "Now can you tell me where the heck we are?"

"North of Denver. At about 15,000 feet."

The tiny space she was in jostled and dipped. Her stomach rose to her throat. "15,000 feet? In the air?"

"Don't panic. I have hundreds of hours' flying experience."

Despite the hammering protest of her head, Erin struggled to sit up and take stock of her situation. "Oh God."

She was in a small propeller plane from the looks of it. And Alec was alone at the controls. She fought the swell of nausea and anxiety that swamped her. "Wh-why am I here? Where are you taking me?" She heard the shrill note in her voice but didn't care.

"Easy, sweetcakes. I've got everything under control."

"That doesn't answer my question!"

Deep breath. Slow exhale. The exercise didn't help. Her nerves still jangled, and her stomach pitched.

"Alec, why am I in this plane? *How* did I get on this plane? I thought you were taking me to a hotel!"

He angled another look over his shoulder. "Anyone ever tell you that you sleep like the dead? I decided I'd get fewer arguments from you if I didn't wake you until we were in the air."

"*You're* kidnapping me now?" She gaped at him, stunned by his stunt.

"Trust me. It's better this way. Because of your concussion—a minor one, the doc assures me—you needed someone to watch you for the next day or two."

Erin's heart gave a little kick. She hadn't had anyone looking out for her interests in a very long time.

"But I had to get out of town, shake the men who've been following me." Alec returned his attention to the dials and gauges in front of him. "At the safe house, I'll have the facilities to start tracking Daniel and protect you at the same time."

She grabbed the back of Alec's seat as the plane jolted through another air pocket. "So why are these men following you? What do they want?"

Alec didn't answer.

"Can you at least tell me which side of the law you're on? Are you one of the good guys?"

He shrugged. "Depends who you ask. We're getting close. Better get ready to go."

Erin shifted to look out the front windshield at the mountainous terrain. "I don't see any airstrip. Where are we supposed to land?"

"We're not landing."

A prickle started at the base of Erin's neck. "Pardon me?"

"We're jumping. I only had one chute in the plane, so I picked up a tandem harness before we took off."

Pinpricks of dread crept down her spine. "We're *jumping?* As in parachuting? As in... No!" A cold sweat beaded on her lip as an image of Bradley's final moments flashed in her mind. "No, Alec! I can't!"

He flipped some switches and slid out from behind the controls. "Fine. Stay on the plane. Although you only have a couple minutes' worth of fuel. Do you know how to land a Cessna?"

"No. I—" Erin's breathing grew ragged, and her heart clambered. "A couple minutes of fuel? But if we jump, the plane—"

"Crashes. I know. That's the point. With luck, the people after us will believe we're dead." Alec stepped over her toward the back cargo area of the tiny plane.

"But—" Erin's head pounded, and her mind spun.

This was a nightmare. No, worse than a nightmare. This was real.

"Please, Alec. There's got to be another way to do this! I can't jump!"

"You'll be strapped to me. Perfectly safe. I've done this dozens of times." He handed her a nylon mesh harness. "Put this on."

Bile burned her throat, and she swallowed hard, searching for her voice. "Alec, wait! You don't understand. Bradley died—"

A screeching siren from the controls interrupted her. "Low fuel! Low fuel!"

"This is our stop." Alec cinched a strap tighter across his chest, then looked at the harness still in her hand. "You coming or not?"

Erin scrambled to don the device, and Alec stepped closer to show her how to arrange the straps and clips. "Please, don't make me do this, Alec! Stay with me! Turn the plane around and land it somewhere. I can't do this!"

He tested one of her straps with a firm tug. Then, grasping her shoulders with strong hands, he met her eyes with his piercing blue gaze. "Yes, you can. I'll be right there with you the whole time. I won't let you get hurt."

His assurances echoed with a distant familiarity. Her stomach lurched. "That's what Bradley always said."

Alec forcibly quashed the sympathy that stirred in him when he looked in Erin's terror-stricken eyes. "Turn around so I can hook up your harness."

She squeezed her eyes shut, and a tear leaked onto her cheek. The sight of that tear as she dutifully complied with his directive landed a sucker punch in his gut.

He had to shove down his reactions to Erin and focus on the jump, focus on getting them both safely to the ground. Drawing a cleansing breath, Alec slid a hand around her waist and pulled her back against him. With his hand splayed on her belly, he held her in place while he fastened the D-rings of her harness to his. With effort, he shut out the sweet scent of her hair, the odd firmness and round swell of her stomach, the shudder that shimmied through her.

"Alec," she said, her voice trembling, "It has to be dangerous for a woman in my condition to—"

"You'll be fine. I'll protect your head when we land."

"I don't mean—"

"Time to go. Walk with me." He nudged her forward. Opened the rear cargo door. Braced as the slipstream roared into the plane.

"Alec!"

"We jump on three! One…two…"

"Alec!"

"Three!"

Chapter 3

After their canopy opened with a crisp snap, Erin opened her eyes and drank in the view of sprawling mountains, the terra-cotta sunset, and the bushy evergreens dotting the jagged slopes of the Rockies. *Beautiful.*

She inhaled the pine-scented air and felt the tension in her muscles seep away. The spectacular view, the exhilarating freedom as they floated on a pillow of air was heady stuff. Despite her fears, every adventure Bradley had taken her on had given her something she treasured. She came away from each challenge energized with the joy of being alive.

The joy of being alive...

In a flash, the thrill of their descent evaporated, replaced with chilling memories of the last trip she'd made with Bradley, the trip that had left her bereft and alone. Erin tensed every muscle and turned her attention from the sunset to their rapid approach to terra firma. Rather, toward a stand of lodgepole pines.

"Alec, we're headed for those trees!" Erin gripped Alec's arm, digging her fingers into his hard muscles, as he toggled their parachute toward the hillside below. She could barely hear herself over the swoosh of blood in her ears and the adrenaline-charged cadence of her heart.

"We're fine, sweetcakes." His voice was irritatingly calm and assured.

When they landed, she was going to deck him for putting her through this.

"Right on target," he crooned.

"You're *aiming* for the trees?"

She felt the vibration of his answering grunt against her back, reverberating in her own chest as if they were one.

"Of course not. I'm gonna set us down in that clearing to the left. When we land, bend your knees—"

"And roll. I know. I've done this before." But when she'd parachuted with Bradley, she hadn't had a throbbing knot on her head or memories of her husband's death replaying in her mind like a film clip looped to repeat ad nauseam.

"You've been skydiving before?" Alec sounded truly shocked.

"A couple times. With Bradley."

They glided over the treetops, and she heard Alec's smug hum of satisfaction, imagined the I-told-you-so gleam in his eyes. As they sailed smoothly to earth, Erin readied herself for landing as Bradley had taught her. Alec wrapped his arm around the top of her head and held it securely against him, protecting her head from further injury as he'd promised he would.

Her feet met the rocky ground with a jarring thud, and her knees buckled. She tried to roll as Alec had instructed, but he lunged the opposite direction. She was hauled with him in a tumbling heap, falling awkwardly on top of him, butt first.

Alec groaned. "I told you to roll!"

"I tried to, but you went the other way! Next time, be more specific about direction."

He snorted. "Roger that, sweetcakes."

She heard the click of metal, and the pressure of the straps restraining her loosened. With a firm shove, Alec scooted her off him and sat up. Erin crawled to her hands and knees and stayed there while she fought for control over her ragged breathing and scampering nerves.

Alec cupped her chin in his hand and brought her head up. "Look at me."

She did, jolting again when her eyes connected with the stunning color and intensity of his. The warmth of his hand on her chin and steadiness of his gaze made her pulse stagger for reasons that had nothing to do with their perilous jump from the airplane.

"Pupils are still normal and even," he said matter-of-factly.

A twinge of disappointment plucked her. The intent of his touch, his level look was clinical, not comforting. Yet he didn't release her chin. "You all right?"

"I'll live."

The corner of his mouth twitched. The closest thing to a smile she'd ever seen cross his face. "See. That wasn't so bad."

She scoffed.

His thumb stroked her cheek, and ribbons of warm sensation streaked from the spot he caressed to pool in her core.

"I know you were scared, but you did great. Good job, sweetcakes."

Erin sighed and tugged her chin from his grasp. "Stop calling me that. My name is Erin, not sweetcakes."

His expression hardening, Alec squared his shoulders and started unfastening the parachute straps crisscrossing his chest.

"Roger that." His tone was as biting as the rocks cutting into her knees.

She tugged at her own harness, wondering where the chastisement about his moniker for her came from. She'd never detected any condescension when he used the name, and she could think of plenty of things worse than *sweetcakes* he could call her. Hormones, she supposed. She'd been emotional and moody a lot lately.

"Who's Bradley?"

Erin snapped her head up. "What?"

"You said you'd parachuted before with Bradley. Is he your brother?"

"I'm an only child. Bradley was my husband."

Alec hesitated before tossing aside his parachute harness. He lifted one black eyebrow. "Was?"

The usual twist of grief squeezed her chest. "He…died two years ago."

The grim slash of Alec's mouth softened. "I'm sorry."

"Yeah. Me, too."

Alec balled the parachute and stuffed it in its pack along with the riser cords and his harness. "Let's get moving. We still have two miles to hike, and it'll be dark soon."

"Two miles?" She gaped at Alec as he hoisted the parachute pack onto his back.

He gave a quick nod. "Uphill. If you're not up to it—"

"What? You'll leave me here to fend for myself?" She crossed her arms over her chest and glared at him.

His scowl returned, and before he turned his back, she thought she saw a flicker of pain in his eyes. "If I were going to leave you behind, I'd have done that long ago. But since we've come this far, it looks like I'm stuck with you for the foreseeable future."

Erin raised her chin and fought back the sting of tears. *Darned hormones!* She didn't want to cry in front of Mr. Macho. "I didn't ask to be involved in your problems! Or to have my life turned upside down by men who want to get at you through me!"

He glanced over his shoulder and sighed. His stony expression relaxed a crumb, though whether from resignation or remorse, Erin couldn't be sure.

"You're right. You're in danger because of me. So I will do everything I can to protect you. But I have other objectives that need attention, and I won't coddle or babysit you."

She bristled. "I don't need a babysitter."

"Good." He started climbing the steep slope. "If the hike is too difficult for you—" he paused and gave her an as-I-was-saying look "—I'll carry you."

His offer caught Erin off guard, landed square in her chest, leaving her speechless. Humbled. She had no doubt this man of many talents and reckless daring could carry her any distance he needed. She'd seen the ease with which he'd lifted the SUV driver at the storage building and had admired Alec's muscular chest and arms from the first day she laid eyes on him.

And he'd obviously already carried her from the SUV to the plane while she slept. The idea taunted her. She had no business entertaining thoughts of getting close to a man with a lifestyle as full of danger as Alec's, but there it was. His drop-dead physique, shocking blue eyes and breathtaking heroics on her behalf were a potent mix.

"I can handle two miles." She fell in step behind him, sticking close despite his quick pace. The sinking sun drew the shadows of the trees and mountaintops in ever-deepening pockets of darkness. The sound of her own labored breaths—Alec didn't seem winded in the least, darn him—blended with the crack of twigs and shuffle of leaves as nocturnal creatures stirred in the settling night.

The frosty bite of the air at this higher elevation burrowed to Erin's bones. Before long, she couldn't control the chattering of her teeth or the shivering in her limbs. "H-how much farther? I'm fr-freezing."

Alec stopped and faced her. "Not far."

He raked a measuring scrutiny over her and stepped toward her. "How's your head?"

She opened her mouth to answer, but he chose that moment to wrap his arms around her and pull her close to his chest. He chafed his hands along her arms and back in brisk strokes. With her nose pressed against his chest, the tangy scent of soap and man surrounding her and his calloused hands moving over her, all rational thought fled. She leaned into him and closed her eyes. Relying on Alec for support and warmth seemed as natural as breathing.

Even with her nap earlier, she was bone-tired, and she savored the chance to rest. She knew fatigue was normal for a woman in her condition, even *before* factoring in the kind of emotional and physical extremes she'd been through today.

"Erin?" Grasping her shoulders, he pushed her to arm's length, and she lamented the lost warmth of his body against hers. He peered down at her, his eyes cutting like lasers through the gathering darkness. "Can you make it just a little farther? The entrance to the safe house is just over the next ridge."

"Is there anything to eat at this safe house?"

He grunted. "The food thing again? Do you *always* eat this much?"

His sarcasm nettled her. After all, she'd tried several times to explain the reason behind her huge appetite, and he'd been so busy ordering her around, he hadn't listened. She brushed past him. "I promise not to eat more than my share."

She heard the scuff of rocks as he followed her up the hill.

"I keep a couple months' supply of food up here along with clothes, ammunition, batteries. Whatever I think I might need."

A chill that had nothing to do with the cold tingled down her spine. "Ammunition?"

"I have to be prepared for anything." His grim tone and

stark warning were reminder enough of his dubious, dangerous existence. And the jeopardy she was in by association with him.

Hardly the peaceful, low-profile life she'd imagined for herself when she moved to Cherry Creek.

They cleared a grouping of trees, and the fading sunlight cast a dim glow over a deep crevasse and the moss-speckled granite face of the mountain on the other side.

Erin looked left and right. The trail, such as it was, seemed to hit a dead end. "Which way?"

"Straight," he said, moving around her and toward the narrow ravine.

She gave him a humorless laugh. Fatigue, cold and her pounding head were making her sick to her stomach again. "Um, in case you missed it…there's a big gulch there."

"Mmm-hmm. That's why there's a bridge." Alec started down the slope toward the ravine.

"There is?" She inched forward but saw nothing except a few ropes strung across the gaping space to the rocky slope on the other side. A knowing quiver started in her gut. *No.*

"Don't tell me those sorry, rotten-looking bits of twine are the bridge you're talking about!"

But before she'd finished protesting, Alec put one foot on the bottom rope and gave it a test bounce. The *bridge* creaked but held his weight. "It'll hold. You go first."

Laughter borne of terror and disbelief bubbled up from her chest. "You're crazy! There's got to be another way across."

Heaving a sigh that said she was wearing on his patience, Alec's shoulders drooped, and he scrubbed a hand over his face. "It's like this, swee…uh…Erin. In about five minutes, it will be completely dark. You won't be able to see where you're putting your feet. This bridge is the only way to get to the safe house, and I, for one, don't intend to freeze my butt off out here after dark." He climbed up to where she stood again and tipped his head toward the ropes. "We don't have time for you to be a chicken about this."

Her spine straightened. "Excuse me! I'll have you know that I've—"

Alec clapped a hand over her mouth. "Spare me the indignant tirade and hustle your pretty buns out there before we lose all our daylight."

She glared at him. She was no chicken! She'd hung with Bradley on even the wildest of his adventures. Just because she voiced a bit of skepticism and wanted to explore other options didn't mean she was chicken!

Pulling away from his grip, she peered over the edge of the crevasse into the fathomless shadows. Her heartbeat skittered. *Bock, bock.* Okay, so she was a little scared. But Bradley used to tell her a little fear was good. It kept you sharp, alert, careful.

"Hold the top ropes for balance, and take it slow and steady."

She snorted. "No kidding."

Trembling so hard she was sure her tremors alone would throw her off balance, Erin eased out on the taut rope. She focused on the few inches right in front of her and nothing else. Despite the frigid temperatures, sweat beaded on her face, her back.

One step. One more. On some level, she was aware of the soothing tone of Alec's voice behind her. He maintained a litany of encouragement, talking her across, praising her every step. His baritone voice lulled her and filtered deep into the cracks in her soul.

When she reached the far side and had scrambled several feet from the edge, her gelatin legs collapsed beneath her. Erin hugged her knees to her chest and gasped deep breaths of icy air, while part of her gave an exulted leap of triumph. She'd done it. She watched Alec cross the ropes in five easy strides, barely wobbling on the swaying ropes. A stroll in the park for him. She groaned. Was there anything this man couldn't do? Once across the ropes, Alec dug in the parachute pack and pulled out a collapsible knife, flicking open the blade.

Erin frowned. "What are you—?"

She gasped as he sawed through the first rope and let it fall into the crevasse. Then the next. And the next.

"What did you do that for? How are we supposed to cross that ravine without the ropes?"

"We're not," he said flatly. He closed the knife and stood. "But neither will anyone else, without a lot of trouble. Which is the point." He offered her a hand up, but she only gaped at him, at the severed ropes.

"Then how—?"

"Trust me, okay? I know what I'm doing."

The adrenaline crash, her surging hormones, her fatigue ganged up on her. Tears stung her eyes. "I just want to go home."

She hated crying in front of him but couldn't seem to stop. Heck, even television commercials for jewelry stores made her weepy these days.

Alec stooped over and lifted her into his arms. He cradled her against his chest and murmured reassurances under his breath. "For the next several days, this is home. Let's get you inside and fix us something hot to eat."

Erin glanced over her shoulder, over Alec's shoulder. "Inside where? I don't see any house."

"That's intentional." Alec ducked his head and started into a night-darkened cave—or rather a wide crack in the granite face of the mountain.

Erin stiffened and huddled closer to Alec's chest. Spelunking was the one thing Bradley had never convinced her to try. The tight, dark tunnels, the tomblike atmosphere, *the bats,* pushed the boundaries of her sense of adventure.

"Alec?" Her voice echoed hollowly in the damp blackness.

"I'm gonna put you down over here just long enough to—"

She twitched as he set her down on the cold rock floor.

"Easy."

"H-have I told y-you how much I h-hate you for p-putting me through this?" Her teeth chattered in the chill.

"So noted." She heard him grunt, heard a loud scrape. A thud. A creak. "I'll be right back."

"Alec!"

"I'm gonna turn on the power, get some lights on for you." Her breath hung in her lungs. "L-lights are g-good."

In the total darkness, she couldn't tell where he'd gone, but moments later a light poured up from a hole in the ground. She scuttled over and peered down a ladder into a cavernous room below. Alec appeared at the foot of the ladder and looked up at her. "Need help coming down?"

The promise of warmth, of food, of safety was all the encouragement she needed. "No. I can do it."

Erin clambered down the ladder and turned to take in the amazing room she was in. Burrowed out of the mountain, buried inside the rocks and soil, the one large room had been filled with computer equipment and electronic gadgetry, stocked with crates of nonperishable food and furnished with a cushiony couch, overstuffed chairs and brass reading lamps. Area rugs in masculine blues and dark reds dotted the hardwood floor. Dark paneled cabinets and framed maps lined the walls.

"Welcome," Alec said, striding toward the galleylike kitchen area. *"Mi casa es su casa."*

Erin could only goggle at the incredible room, hidden inside the mountain. "You live *here?*"

"Only when necessary. Beef stew or chili mac?" He held out two cans for her inspection.

Her stomach rumbled. "Stew, please."

With a nod, he set the can on the counter and took down a pan to heat their dinner.

Though she could feel warm air stirring in the room, she rubbed her arms to chase the lingering chill of outdoors. "How in the world did you build this place? How did you get all this furniture and equipment up here?"

He thwacked the bottom of the stew can with his palm, emptying it into the pot. "It wasn't easy. But all the trouble and expense were worth it. Daniel and I have used this place a number of times to lie low when we had someone breathing down our necks." Alec tossed the empty can in the trash and sighed. "I'd kinda hoped I'd find him here. But…"

He didn't finish the thought.

She crossed the room and sank tiredly on a tall stool on the opposite side of the kitchen counter. "Tell me about Daniel."

He gave her a startled look, then continued stirring the pot of stew. The savory scent of beef and onion spiced the air, and her mouth watered.

"Daniel was my partner." Alec scowled and grunted. "He *is* my partner. We've worked together for close to five years."

"That's a long time. You must be close."

Alec was silent for long moments, staring into the pot and wearing a contemplative expression. "He's my best friend. My only friend," he said at last. "He went missing nine months ago. I didn't think much of it at first. I mean, he's one of the best agents on the team. He could handle whatever trouble came his way." Alec tapped the spoon on the edge of the pot and faced her. "But when I still hadn't heard from him after five months, I got restless. If he was alive, he'd have gotten some word to me, some message."

"Like the letter that came to my house. The one Knife and his buddy were after."

Alec frowned. "No. Written communication is too danger-ous. As Knife and his cohort proved. It's too easy to trace, leaves evidence that can be used against you. This missive from Daniel is highly irregular and...has me stumped."

"Then you've read his letter?"

"I looked at it while you were having the CT scan."

"And?"

Alec stirred the stew again, then took down two bowls from the cabinet.

"You're not going to tell me what it said, are you?"

"Sharing information is not part of my job description. Leaks get people killed."

"What is it exactly that you do?"

"Whatever I'm needed for."

"Can you be more specific?"

"No."

Erin huffed and shook her head. "Who am I gonna tell? What could it hurt to give me some clue who you are and what I'm involved in?"

He filled the emptied pot with water and left it to soak in the sink. Handing her one steaming bowl of stew, he carried the other bowl to a table behind her.

She spun on her stool to face him. "Come on, Alec. You can trust me!"

He arched a dark eyebrow and set his spoon down. "Oh? *'Alec has the letter. He just left. In a florist's van,'*" Alec said in a poor imitation of her voice. "Ring a bell?"

She cringed and gritted her teeth. "That's different!"

"Really? How?"

"I wasn't going to let them kill me over that stupid letter!"

"So I can trust you as long as your life's not at stake. Is that the size of it?"

"I... Oh, forget it!" Her injured temple gave a painful throb as she stabbed a bit of potato from her bowl and jabbed it in her mouth. And scalded her tongue. "Ow!"

"Careful, it's hot," Alec said, the quirk of his eyebrow the only outward change in his expressionless facade.

She tossed him a glare, then turned her back.

"It wasn't a letter. It was a map," Alec said a few minutes later. "Other than telling me he's alive, I've got no idea what Daniel's reasoning was for sending it. It's got to have some significance, but as yet, I've not come up with much."

Erin saw the morsel of information for what it was. A gift. A show of faith. A proffered truce. Perhaps even a request for help.

She shoveled a carrot in her mouth and licked the gravy from the spoon before carrying her bowl to the table to join Alec. "What kind of map?"

"A treasure map. Like a kid might get as a souvenir at the pirate ride at the fair."

Erin's brain began processing, clicking through what pieces of information she knew. "A pirate map. And didn't you say you call him Lafitte? Wasn't Lafitte a pirate who lived near New Orleans around 1812?"

Alec nodded. "I called Daniel Lafitte because he was from Louisiana. He called me Blackbeard."

"Blackbeard." She smiled. "Why?"

He scratched the dark stubble on his chin. "I'd think that was obvious."

"Oh. Right." She felt somehow disappointed there wasn't a more intriguing reason behind Alec's nickname. She took another bite of stew, then, mouth full, she asked, "Why pirate names?"

Alec pushed his empty bowl away and rubbed a hand on his flat stomach. "Because that's how we saw ourselves. The rogue element—tempting fate, flirting with disaster, answering only to ourselves." His mesmerizing blue eyes locked on her. "Often operating outside the law."

An uneasy itch inched down her spine. "You're criminals?"

He rocked his head from one side to the other and rubbed the muscles at the base of his neck. "Not exactly. We work for Uncle Sam, protecting U.S. interests, but our modus operandi sometimes crosses into a…*gray* area."

Erin met his level gaze, and the stew in her stomach suddenly felt like rocks. "I've read about so called 'black ops' that the government conducts. Highly classified operations with no formal budget, no paper or electronic record, no particular departmental jurisdiction. Operations conducted in a way that they can be completely denied, no proof available of their existence." She swallowed hard. "Is that what you do? What I'm in the middle of?"

Alec didn't so much as blink. But his silence spoke volumes.

"Oh God," she mumbled, feeling the contents of her stomach roil and rebel. She dashed to the sink and lost her dinner down the drain. Drawing a slow breath, she battled for her composure, struggled to make sense of the bizarre twist her life had taken today. With shaking hands, she turned on the water to rinse her mouth and splash her face.

Cool fingers brushed her cheek, pulling her hair back from her face. She peeked up at Alec, who stared at her with a furrow of concern puckering his brow. "You sure you don't have a virus?"

She closed her eyes, weak, weary and more than a little frightened of the mess she was in. "I'm sure. Just a case of black-op-induced indigestion, complicated by morning sickness that, in fact, lasts all day."

His hand tightened slightly at her nape, and she lifted her head to meet his puzzled frown.

"I've been trying to tell you all day, but there always seemed to be a thug to chase or a plane to jump out of at just the wrong moment."

She watched as some of the color leached from Alec's face.

He could jump from the top of a moving truck, parachute into mountainous terrain and cross a rickety rope bridge without flinching, but *this* had him blanching. She almost laughed.

But she didn't. She took her baby's life very seriously.

"You're pregnant?" he rasped.

Erin raised her chin a notch and slipped a hand over her belly. "Fourteen weeks."

Chapter 4

*P*regnant.

Alec dragged a hand down his jaw and studied the woman asleep on one of the two twin-size Murphy beds. In sleep, Erin Bauer seemed all the more vulnerable. Especially with the blue-black knot near her hairline.

An uncomfortable prick of conscience arrowed through him. His responsibility to protect her was all the greater knowing her condition, knowing he was protecting two lives rather than just one. Knowing the arduous paces he'd put her through to get to the hideout. He'd made a pregnant woman jump from an airplane, for crying out loud! He shifted restlessly in his chair and tried to tamp the rising guilt. He hadn't known. How could he have known?

Alec sighed and spun his chair back toward the computer screen, where he searched the internet for venues that sold souvenir maps like the one Daniel had sent him.

You should have figured it out.

Erin had tried to tell him she was pregnant, but he'd been so single-minded in his determination to get to the safe house, he'd not listened to her. Hadn't paid attention to the signs, the warning flags—Erin's ready tears and testiness, her voracious appetite and disproportionate fatigue.

And the odd tightness of her slightly rounded belly when he'd held her in place to fasten her tandem jump harness to his.

Warmth flooded his veins remembering the soft crush of her backside against him, the vanilla scent that clung to her, and how her shudder of fear had ricocheted through his body and shaken his heart. Simply remembering made his body tighten and his pulse quake.

What was happening to him? Every crumb of his training seemed to fly out the window when he was around Erin—a fact he needed to correct if he intended to keep her and her baby alive. Even now a niggle of something plucked at his brain. Something about her pregnancy that didn't add up. Something she'd told him…but what?

Alec puffed out a staccato breath and concentrated on the list of retailers on the monitor. The companies that sold the pirate's map were spread across the country. Daniel could have gotten the map from any of these places, could have even ordered one of the silly maps from the internet. Not a lot of help there. Alec hit Print, and with a click and a whir, a hard copy of the retailers' addresses slid out of the machine beside him.

"What's that?" Erin asked.

He spun his chair around and found her blinking groggily at the monitor. Wearing one of his T-shirts and rumpled from sleep, she shouldn't have looked so damn sexy. But she did.

Alec squeezed the armrests of his computer chair and forcibly reined in his libido. "Just a little research on where this map may have come from. I'm sorry if the light woke you."

She raked loose caramel-colored curls off her forehead and yawned. "Naw. I had to go." She flashed him a wry grin.

"Seems all I do nowadays is eat and pee." She shrugged. "Not that I didn't know what I was getting myself into. I gave my decision to get pregnant plenty of thought."

As she staggered toward the bathroom, her comment tugged at his brain, prodding him. Her decision? What about the father's say? But she'd said her husband had died....

Two years ago.

Alec sat straighter in his chair. He'd just assumed her late husband was the father, but obviously Erin had someone else in her life as recently as three months ago. Alec watched Erin emerge from the bathroom and drop limply to the bed, refusing to give in to the bite of jealousy when he thought of Erin in some other man's arms. "Your boyfriend is bound to miss you before long, maybe report your disappearance to the police."

Alec grimaced. *Not too subtle, Kincaid.*

Erin's brow puckered. "I don't have a boyfriend."

Oh? A pathetically juvenile elation flared inside him.

"I, uh…just assumed the baby's father might be—"

"*Bradley* is my baby's father." She squared her shoulders and pressed a hand to her belly. "No one is going to miss me, I'm afraid." She yawned again. "Welcome to twenty-first-century medicine, Mr. Kincaid. I got pregnant in a doctor's office with Bradley's wedding present to me."

Alec lifted an eyebrow. "His wedding present?"

Erin slid off the bed and padded across the floor. She pulled up the computer chair Daniel used when the two of them stayed at the safe house together. Tucking her bare foot under her, she gave Alec a sleepy smile. "Yeah. I asked him to make a deposit, as it were, to a sperm bank before we married. I knew I wanted children, lots of them, and I was afraid…" She stopped and wrapped her arms around her chest, a self-defensive gesture that stirred Alec's protective instincts.

"When I was three, my dad was in a car wreck that left him paralyzed and…unable to father any more children. My parents were crushed. They'd planned on a big family and couldn't have it." She rubbed the goose bumps that dotted her arms, and Alec had to grip the edge of his chair to stop himself from pulling her into his lap and rubbing warmth into her himself.

Erin's brow puckered in thought. "Bradley was an adrenaline junkie. He loved to test his limits, try new things, live on the edge. I knew that going into our marriage, but I worried about him suffering an injury that would keep us from having the children we wanted. Like what happened to my dad." Moisture sparkled in her eyes, and an answering sympathy grabbed Alec by the throat. "So I asked Bradley to…*insure our future* as a gift to me before we married. And he did. I used his wedding present, which had been in deep freeze at a clinic, to get pregnant. It took three tries—" she pushed out of Daniel's chair and paced past him, leaving her vanilla scent in her wake "—but I'm having Bradley's baby."

Alec cleared his throat. "It takes a lot of courage to raise a child alone."

She pivoted on her toes to face him. "Courage? I don't know. I just knew how much I wanted a child to hold, to nurture. To love."

An uneasy prickle chased through his chest. He'd spent the better part of the past twelve hours lusting after a woman who was carrying her dead husband's child. And while that fact should have dumped ice water on the fire licking his veins, instead the confounding pull she had with him merely shifted, kicking harder. The mysterious power Erin had to distract him from his training and his duty burrowed deeper and left him struggling for a breath. *Not good.*

As she yawned again, her gaze drifted to the computer printout. "Can I help with that?"

Alec shoved out of his chair and took her by the elbow,

directing her back to the bed. "I'm almost finished for the night. Get some sleep."

"If you change your mind, I don't mind helping."

"I'll remember that." He walked back over to the computer and powered it down for the night, then carried the list of retailers to the sofa. He stretched his legs out and glanced through the addresses once more before clicking off the light and closing his eyes.

The gentle sough of Erin's breathing reached through the darkness. The subtle intimacy of listening to her sigh softly in sleep wrapped around him, made his body buzz with restrained desire. Sharing these cramped quarters with Erin, a woman he had no right wanting, a distraction he couldn't afford indulging, would likely drive him insane, one vanilla-scented sigh at a time.

"Did you know that at fourteen weeks, a fetus has already developed his own unique fingerprint?" Erin asked the next morning as she restlessly paced the bunker. She glanced to the computer console where Alec had worked all morning, ignoring her attempts at conversation, his fingers flying across the keyboard. She remembered the tenderness of those same hands when he'd checked her pulse, swept the hair from her face when she got sick, and held her chin as he examined her pupils. Skilled hands that had, in all likelihood, been used for all sorts of shadowy, questionable deeds. Had he ever killed anyone in his secretive line of work? She hated thinking of Alec pulling the trigger on the gun he'd produced yesterday or using his strength to snap a neck. She shoved the thought aside for more pleasant topics. "My baby already has eye-lashes, toenails, ears—"

Alec lifted his hands from the keyboard, and the mesmer-izing clickity-clack, that for hours had been his only response to her questions, fell silent. "Would you please stop pacing? It's making me crazy."

"I could, but then boredom would make me nuts," she returned. "Oh, wait! It already is."

He turned toward her for the first time in hours. Judging from the creases that crinkled around his eyes and his generally sullen mood, she guessed he hadn't slept well. "Entertainment isn't a priority when Daniel or I come up here. Doing our job is about all we have time for."

Compunction for her sarcasm bit Erin hard, and her shoulders sagged. "Sorry. I'm just not used to having so much time on my hands. Can't I help with anything you're doing?"

Alec glanced over his shoulder at the computer monitor and pursed his lips. "You know how to hack into Interpol's database?"

Erin scoffed. "No."

"Then I don't think you'll be any help to me." He spun his chair back to the computer and resumed tapping the keyboard.

Ridiculous. She was cooped up here with Mr. Dour Spy Guy while a man who'd threatened to slit her throat waltzed around free as a bird. A circumstance she refused to accept.

She marched over to Alec and braced her hands on her hips. "Do you at least have a blank piece of paper and a pencil?"

He gave her his one-raised-eyebrow look, which she'd already learned meant *What's going on in your head?*

"If I do, does it mean you'll stop prattling about low-carbohydrate recipes and fetal development, and let me work in peace?"

She huffed. "I'm not prattling!"

He grimaced and lifted a hand to forestall her argument. "I just work better if I don't have someone...*talking* to me all the time. I need quiet."

"Not a multitasker, eh?"

He cocked his head slightly and narrowed his eyes. "I'll show you later how well I *multitask* when it's called for. As for paper and pencils, try that drawer under the scanner. Now can I please finish what I'm doing?"

With an exasperated sigh, she twisted her fingers over her lips as if locking them and tossing away the key. After retrieving the supplies she needed, she curled her feet under her on the sofa and began sketching from memory the face of the man who'd threatened her life yesterday. For close to an hour, she smudged lines with her thumb here and erased there, shaping, shading and retracing until she had a good likeness.

Satisfied with her efforts, she carried her drawing over to Alec, who had finished pounding the keyboard several minutes earlier. Now he simply stared at the treasure map Daniel had sent him as if the paper would eventually yield all the secrets of the universe.

"Here." She extended her sketch of Knife to him and squared her shoulders. "I don't know if this will help catch him or not, but I was tired of sitting back doing nothing after the terror he put me through."

Alec took the proffered sheet and held it at arm's length to study it. The hard lines in his face softened in surprise, and he raised his gaze to her. "Not bad. You're no police department sketch artist, but for an amateur, this is good."

Erin folded her arms over her chest and scowled at his backhanded compliment while he examined the drawing some more. Setting the picture aside, he rocked his computer chair back and faced her. "Where'd you learn to sketch like that?"

"No lessons. Just naturally talented." She cocked one hip out and presented him with a smug grin. "Of course, I got lots of practice drawing faces in college when I worked a couple summers as the official sketch artist for my hometown sheriff's department."

Alec opened and closed his mouth like a fish, then frowned. "Touché."

Erin pulled the other chair closer and dropped on the edge of the seat. "Can you use it with all your spy stuff to at least find out who he is?"

"Let's see." He snatched the sketch up, and with a shove of his feet, he rolled his chair to another counter, where a flat-bed scanner and printer sat. He slapped the drawing into the scanner, punched a few buttons, then rolled back to his keyboard. A minute later, Erin's drawing of Knife was on Alec's computer screen and rapid-fire images scrolled next to it.

"What's happening?"

"I've asked the computer to compare the drawing to images of known criminals from police files around the world."

"How long will this take?"

"Well, we could cut the time considerably if we cross-referenced with a few other variables." Alec hit a button, and the images stopped scrolling. "We know his weapon of choice was a Bowie hunting knife with a nine-inch blade," he said as he typed this information in.

Erin leaned closer, an eager excitement pumping through her blood. "The driver called him Manny a couple times, and I remember him having a scar on his arm." She paused and mentally recreated the position with which Knife had held her. "On his left arm, the one he held me with."

"Good," Alec said as he entered this information, as well. "This is good. What else?"

"Well, if he used his right hand to hold the knife, wouldn't that make him right-handed? Does that help?"

The corner of Alec's mouth twitched, hinting at a grin. "Everything helps. You never know what piece of information will help you snag your target. I caught a guy in Australia once simply because I knew what brand of socks he wore."

He sent every bit of information the two of them could

remember about Knife and his partner to the computer data-base and clicked Search. Scooting away from the desk, Alec stood and stretched his arms and back.

Erin watched the play of muscle and sinew as Alec worked the stiffness from his body and couldn't stop the flip-flop sensation in her chest. For a man whose body left no secret to his strength and deadly potential, Alec had shown her decided gentleness in the past twenty-four hours. His careful touch when he checked her vitals spoke of a man who could be as tender as he could be rough.

Alec strolled toward the kitchen. "While the program runs through all the files, how about lunch? You hungry?"

"Did yesterday teach you nothing?" A heady sense of accomplishment for their shared efforts that morning flowed through Erin, energizing her, and she reclaimed her stool at the kitchen counter. "I need to eat a little something every couple hours or I get sick to my stomach. My doctor said it's because the baby is growing so fast."

He hummed in acknowledgment. "Fingerprints, toenails and eyelashes already at fourteen weeks."

She felt a smile blossom on her face. "You *were* listening!"

Another quirk at the corner of his mouth. "And you said I couldn't multitask."

Erin propped her chin on her hand and leaned her elbows on the counter. "Alec, I doubt there's much you *can't* do."

Across the room, the computer beeped. Alec set down the can of soup he'd taken off the shelf and strode over to study the image frozen on the monitor.

Erin leaned to the side trying to see around him. "What is it?"

"William Manny. One of about twelve aliases for Hector Godfrey, gun for hire."

"Gun for hire?" Icy fingers gripped Erin's heart.

"Means he's not the one behind everything that's happened. Also tells me his main objective wasn't to kill either of us, or we'd be dead."

"Then he really did just want the letter. But why?"

"Not the letter, per se. He wants Daniel." Alec faced her, his hands balled at his sides and his glacial eyes glittering with lethal intent. "But I intend to find Daniel first."

"How does a person go about hiring an assassin? Whoever paid William Manny would have to have criminal connections to hire a professional assassin. It's not like your average citizen can look up *hired killers* in the yellow pages and just start getting estimates as if you were having your roof repaired." Erin paused from her monologue long enough to crunch a graham cracker, her third snack that evening.

Alec rubbed his eyes, then blinked away the blur of fatigue. He'd stared at Daniel's map so long and hard, he could barely see straight. And Erin's incessant talking didn't help.

With the exception of her nap that afternoon, the chatterbox had filled his ear all day with her opinions on everything from the economy to Greek revival architecture. Erin was clearly intelligent and well-read, and despite his best intentions to shut out her chatter, he found himself drawn to her commentary, soaking up clues to her personality, her interests, her preferences. Beyond her intellect, Erin's shapely figure and silky curls enticed him, while her dark, expressive eyes and lush mouth turned him inside out. He'd tried hard not to think about kissing her all day. Her distraction could prove deadly if he couldn't get past his unprofessional fascination with her.

"Do you know any assassins?" she asked, her eyes wide with the horror of such a possibility.

If she only knew…

Without answering, Alec ducked his head and worked again at deciphering Daniel's map. His partner hadn't used any of the codes they typically did, hadn't embedded any co-ordinates that Alec could tell.

"What do you think Manny has told the person who hired him? Do you think there's any way they could have followed us up here?"

Flattening his hands on the table with a sigh, Alec pushed his chair back. "I don't know and not likely."

Alec walked over to the closet and pulled his coat off its hanger.

"Where are you going?"

He shoved his arms in the sleeves of the parka, noting the touch of panic in her voice. "Just outside for a minute. I need air." *I need time to think, to clear my head.*

Erin leaped to her feet.

He held a hand up. "I'll be just outside, and I'll be right back. I promise."

He swung away from the hurt and worry that filled her eyes, steeling himself to the unsettling tug her expression caused in his chest. Blast it all, he owed Daniel better than to let a pair of vulnerable eyes sway him from his duty.

Alec sped up the steel ladder rungs and shouldered open the trapdoor to the bunker entrance. The stinging blast of cold night air sobered him quickly, as he'd hoped. Maybe out here, away from Erin's tantalizing vanilla scent teasing him and her angel's voice filling his head, he could plan strategy, fig-ure out what he was missing regarding the mysterious map.

He stalked out into the crisp night and headed toward the rocky overhang directly in front of the cave, from which he had a nearly panoramic view of the surrounding mountains. An ideal lookout point, had he been interested in the view. In-stead, he mulled over the fraction of information he'd gleaned today, largely due to Erin's sketch of Manny.

Many of the questions Erin had voiced that evening were the same ones that nagged him. Who had the means, the motive, the money to hire someone like Manny? Where did Daniel fit in this picture? Alec couldn't shake the feeling Lafitte's disappearance had something to do with the botched attempt to bring in General Ramirez. He hadn't heard from his partner since that fateful day, and Alec had learned not to believe in coincidence.

Jamming his hands in his pockets and hunching his shoulders against the biting breeze, Alec stared into the deep darkness of the night. He replayed the sights and sounds of the Colombian jungle, the spray of gunfire.

There'd been shouting. In Spanish. What had been said?

Behind him, a branch cracked, snapping Alec from his thoughts. He groped at his back for his SIG-Sauer. Flicked off the safety. Another twig cracked. Alec sidled close to a tree and crouched in the shadow. With the gibbous moon as his only light, he aimed his weapon toward the source of the sound. Saw something move.

Something human.

Chapter 5

Alec waited, watched.

He doubted they'd been followed to the mountain bunker. But the area was too inaccessible for the intruder to be a hunter, a camper. Alec fell back on training, keeping his body under cool control, his mind clear. He sharpened his senses, concentrating on his surroundings. Listening to the rustle of leaves. Narrowing his gaze to separate form from shadow. Sniffing the air to smell...*vanilla.*

"Alec? Where are you?"

Suppressing a groan and taming the adrenaline teeming in his blood, Alec stood and moved from behind the tree.

"What are you doing out here, Erin?"

She turned toward him when he spoke and stumbled over loose rocks to join him. "Same as you. Getting some air. I was going stir-crazy in there."

"I almost shot you. I thought you were—" He huffed his frustration. "Do you ever do as you're told?"

"I'm sorry." Erin watched, mesmerized, as Alec's breath frosted in a white cloud as he spoke. He turned his gaze out toward the empty blackness, beyond which she knew jagged mountains surrounded them. But in the pocket of moonlight and chill air, only she and Alec existed.

"Warm enough?" he asked.

"Mmm-hmm. I borrowed some extra shirts from your closet. Hope that's okay."

"Want to see something amazing?" he asked, and she found herself studying the way his lips moved when he talked.

She slid him a lopsided grin. "Sure, Superman. Amaze me."

He reached for her, framing her face with his hands, and tilted her head up.

Erin was still reeling from the heady warmth of his calloused palms on her cheeks when the view registered. Her breath caught. Directly over her head, a wall of clouds rolled in, the promised storm front, but ahead of the clouds the sky was still clear. A million stars, more stars than she'd ever seen, twinkled and blinked down at her. Wispy clouds drifted past a bright, three-quarters moon. "Oh, Alec. How beautiful!"

"Yeah. I was trained to navigate using nothing but the stars. Still, you don't get the full effect unless you get far from civilization, where there are no lights."

Erin glanced at him. "Spend a lot of time away from civilization, do you?"

He jerked his gaze to hers and hesitated as if he'd realized he'd given away some secret. A muscle in his jaw flexed, and he returned his attention to the stars. "Time enough."

Studying the bristles of his unshaven chin and the hard edge of his countenance, she could easily picture Alec roughing it in the outback, cruising the Nile or hiking the slopes of the Andes.

She raised her eyes heavenward again and remembered tranquil nights spent around a campfire with Bradley, wak-

ing on cool mornings in the wilderness with dew clinging to
their tent and frizzing her hair.

"Thank you," she murmured.

"For what?"

"For reminding me how much I used to love this. It's been
a long time since—"

She didn't finish the thought. Alec had made it clear he
hated her chatter, and somehow she didn't feel she was ready
to share that part of her life with him. It still hurt too much.

She caught her lip in her teeth and swallowed the burn of
tears in her throat. If Bradley were here, he'd tell her to let
his death go, to move on with her life and seize every moment. Not hide in a house in Cherry Creek. Not run from a
job she loved because of a tragic mistake.

"Since…?" Alec prompted.

"Since I—" She shook her head.

How could Alec understand the choices she'd made?

His black eyebrows drew into a frown, and he gave her a
long searching look. "Who hurt you, Erin?"

"Forget it. I'd bet you've never run from a problem or hidden away to lick your wounds." Erin tipped her head back to
stare up at the stars again, and for several minutes, the stirring breeze and the click of branches as they swayed were
the only sounds around them. She inhaled the cold air, savoring the moment.

"You're wrong." Alec's low tone drifted to her like a part
of the night. Quiet. Dark. Mysteriously soothing.

She shifted her gaze toward him and found him staring
at her. Moonlight reflected from his azure eyes and started
a hum in her blood.

"I ran from something just tonight. A complication I have
no idea how to handle."

Erin laid a hand on his arm and squeezed. "What, Alec?
I want to help."

He grunted. "I've said too much."

"Maybe the real problem is you haven't said enough. Talk to me, Alec. If I've done something—"

"No." He faced her and gripped her shoulders. Scowled. Sighed. "I want to kiss you."

Oh.

Erin opened her mouth to answer him, but her breath backed up in her lungs.

"Don't worry," Alec said, his expression rigid, tightly reined. "I won't."

"Why not?" The question popped out before she could stop it.

His eyebrow arched. "What?"

Squaring her shoulders, she followed impulse, tossed down the gauntlet, prepared to face the consequences later. "Why can't you kiss me?"

His hands tightened on her shoulders, and his expression shifted, clearly regrouping mentally.

"Because I…I…"

This stammering, somewhat uncertain Alec made her smile. She'd shocked her can-do-anything rescuer, found a crack in superknight's armor.

Tilting her chin higher, she stepped closer, near enough for the white cloud of her breath to mingle with his. "What if I were to kiss you?"

She knew the exact moment he made his decision. His gaze dipped to her mouth, and the determined blaze returned to his eyes. Resolve firming his rugged features, he slid a hand up her neck to cradle the base of her skull and drew her closer.

Anticipation crackled in her every synapse, and she rose on her toes to bring her lips to his.

Alec breathed her name as he captured her mouth and reclaimed command of the situation. His lips were warm against her night-chilled skin, and she tasted cinnamon and need in his kiss. She clung to the front of his parka as he angled his head and increased the pressure of his mouth. He drew greedily on her lips, and his tongue swept inside and tangled with hers.

A dizzying blend of lethargy and pleasure thrummed through her limbs, her mind. Like the man, Alec's kiss combined power and finesse, strength and tenderness in perfect balance.

Heat seeped to her core, and for precious moments, she felt safe. Cherished. Complete.

All too soon for her liking, Alec groaned and tore his mouth from hers. Stepped back.

For several seconds, she struggled to catch her breath and returned his penetrating stare. Alec looked as shell-shocked as she felt.

The sting of something icy and wet on her cheeks finally snapped her from the spellbinding lure of his gaze. Erin tipped her face toward the stars and blinked at the flutter of white flakes filling the sky.

A smile tugged at her lips. "It's snowing."

Alec cast a glance around them and held out his hand. "Yeah." His all-business persona returned, body taut and face stern. "We should go in."

"But it's so lovely." She extended her arms and turned slowly as she watched the dainty crystals dance in the air.

Alec cleared his throat. "Erin."

The dark tone of his voice stopped her. She met his troubled frown. "What?"

"That can't happen again. I—" His dark eyebrows knit in consternation. "We can't kiss."

His grave mood took the edge off the warm glow that lingered from his kiss. "Alec?"

"I have a duty to protect you, and I will. But I can't forget that my partner's life may be in danger. I have to find

Daniel without distractions. That's my priority above everything else."

Pain flickered in the eyes that moments ago had been smoky with desire for her. Like flipping a switch, Alec closed himself off, wiping all emotion and ambivalence from his expression and tightening his jaw.

A prick of disappointment stabbed her chest before a voice of reason whispered to her. Despite his rugged appeal, his moments of tenderness, his earthshaking kiss, Alec led a life fraught with unknowns, peril and questionable ethics. She couldn't imagine a man more wrong for her.

She slid a hand to her stomach and swallowed the emotion that choked her. *Her* priority had to be providing safety and stability for her baby. How could she do that with Alec in her life? What kind of example would Alec, with his dangerous job, be to her child? The worst kind.

She knew painfully well what could happen if a child emulated the wrong role model. A shiver unrelated to the winter chill shimmied through her.

"You're cold," Alec said and took her by the arm. "You should head in and thaw out."

In truth, the multiple layers of Alec's clothes kept her amply warm. She didn't bother to correct him, though, since an empty chill had settled in her chest that no quantity of clothing could ever banish. An instinctive sense told her that by protecting her child from Alec's high-risk lifestyle, she was losing a chance at something special.

Kissing Erin had been a colossal mistake, Alec groused mentally the next morning. Even now, hours later, his body vibrated with sexual hunger, and his head pounded with self-recrimination. Whatever it took, he would block Erin from his thoughts today and get some work done. Even if it meant sitting outside in the snow all day. The frigid air would do him good, might even cool the fire that licked his veins.

As if conjured by his thoughts, Erin padded into the kitchen area and raked errant waves of caramel hair from her face. "What time is it?"

His too-big-for-her T-shirt hung lopsided off one of her shoulders, and Alec prepared to battle the weakness in him that had lowered his guard last night. He had to root out the source of his failing and destroy it, before it destroyed him. He dragged his gaze from the rumpled yet oddly enticing vision she was and doggedly focused his attention on the brewing coffee.

"You know, I was thinking," she said, then paused to yawn. "What if the treasure map Daniel sent you is a hoax? Something intended to throw you off a trail you were on."

"I don't think so. Daniel wouldn't do that." Alec crossed his arms over his chest.

Don't look at her. Don't think about how good she smells. Don't remember the wounded look in her eyes when you pushed her away last night.

A fist of regret grabbed his chest and squeezed. The last thing he wanted was to hurt Erin, but his training, his job made relationships with women difficult. Almost impossible.

"It's not impossible." Her comment so closely mirrored his thoughts that he cast a startled gaze toward her.

Daniel's letter. A hoax.

"What's that look for?" Her pert, freckled nose wrinkled, and she tipped her head.

The urge to pull her close and nibble that crinkled nose slammed him in the chest. He swung away from her, biting back an oath.

She harrumphed. "Fine. Whatever. I'm just trying to help. It can't hurt to consider the possibility the letter's a fake."

His back to her, he poured himself a cup of coffee and

knocked back half the mug's contents. The hot liquid scalded his throat on the way down. "If the map were from anyone but Daniel, I might consider that option. But Daniel wouldn't waste time on a joke. Wouldn't send false information."

"You're sure?"

Setting his cup on the counter, he glanced at her. "Positive. Daniel and I shoot straight with each other, no matter what. We work well together because we've built a solid trust. If he sent the map, then he—"

"*If* Daniel sent it? You mean you have some question now if it's even from him?"

He shook his head and carried his mug to the table where the map was spread out. "No. I'm sure it's from Lafitte. But the fact that he sent it, that he contacted me at all, tells me he's run into some kind of problem. That he needs…" Guilt pinched hard. "He needs my help."

What if Daniel had needed him nine months ago in that Colombian jungle? Alec sucked in a deep breath and swiped a hand down his face. No second guessing. He'd done as they agreed. *Every man for himself.*

Still, the idea that Daniel could have been captured, tortured, made Alec crazy. It made him feel vulnerable in a way he didn't like, couldn't explain.

Erin sat in the chair next to him and reached for his hand. She wrapped her fingers around his, yanking him out of his reverie and jolting his senses with her comforting touch. "You miss him, don't you?"

The warm-liquid sound of her voice bathed him, seeped inside him to soothe his taut nerves. Scooting closer, she slid her other hand down his arm. She trapped his hand between hers, lacing her fingers with his and squeezing gently. A zinging heat stirred to life where her hand held his and sang through his blood, spreading through his body.

"You're worried about him. That's why finding him is so important to you. Isn't it?"

He met her mahogany eyes, drinking in the compassion and unnerving insight reflected there. "He's my partner. It's my duty to find him."

She shook her head. "He's more than your partner. He's your friend. You said he was like a brother to you."

Alec sat straighter, an uneasy prickle slithering up his back.

"You'd feel the need to find him even if he weren't your partner," Erin said. "Because you care about him."

Alec tensed and furrowed his brow. "No. It's not like that."

Agents for the black ops team couldn't afford to care. Emotions had no place in the deadly operations and delicate tightrope they walked with enemy forces, double agents, skittish informants and calculating mercenaries. His survival in the cutthroat world of espionage and counterterrorism meant using his brain, his training, his instincts. Emotions muddied the waters and weakened resolve. A moment's hesitation given to remorse or sympathy or misplaced allegiance could prove lethal.

Erin's thumb stroked a hypnotizing pattern on his wrist, and her mouth pulled in a sideways grin. "Alec, I can see it in your face, in your eyes whenever you talk about him. I'm not saying there's anything funny going on between you. But it's obvious he's important to you."

Her caress left him off balance and feeling exposed. How in Hades was he supposed to survive the next several days cooped up on this mountain with her? She distracted him with her every breath, her every smile.

Alec carefully extracted his hand from hers and smoothed the edges of the map. Rather than address her observations regarding Daniel, he ducked his head to study the images, the words he'd already memorized. To no avail. He waved a hand at the map and scowled. "What the hell does all this mean?"

Erin made a raspberry at him and pushed back from the table. "Okay, I can take a hint. Bradley was the same way. Men don't like to talk about their *feelings*. I'll drop it."

"There's nothing to discuss."

As she sauntered back to the kitchen, she cast him an I-don't-buy-that look. "Just as well, since I've been pregnant I've had enough feelings for three people. My hormones are off the charts. I cry over the silliest things."

Great. He was cohabitating with a sexy, *emotional* room-mate. He could defuse a brick of C4 explosives without blinking, but a teary woman left him in a cold sweat. Alec suppressed a groan and picked up the edges of the map. He held the fake parchment up to block his view of long legs and tousled hair.

"Like the other day…" Erin chuckled. "I had a roach in the kitchen. Blech! Nasty little creatures. I squashed it, of course, but then I got all sniffly because maybe that roach had a family that would miss him. I had to laugh at myself. Grieving a roach… Sheesh."

Behind the screen of Daniel's map, Alec lifted a corner of his mouth. Sheesh was right. The tender heart.

And so the gabfest begins for another day.…

Alec blew a slow breath through pursed lips and turned the map ninety degrees to study one of the pictures from a different angle.

"Alec, do the letters l-i-l-x-t-r-a-o-c-o-m mean anything to you?"

He peered over the top of the map and raised an eyebrow. "Should they?"

She pointed to the map and wiggled her finger. "When you hold the paper up like that, those letters show through, like someone traced them in dark ink and it soaked through."

"Really?" A spark of revived hope jump-started his pulse.

"Here, I'll show you." She padded across the floor and slipped the map from his hands. After clicking on the floor lamp by the sofa, she held the map so that it was backlit.

Sure enough, the letters she'd read off stood out when viewing the sheet from the back. Along with a set of lines. Partial tracings of the swirling designs.

"Lilxtraocom?" Alec wrote the letters on a notepad and scratched the two days' growth of stubble on his cheek. "Doesn't ring any bells."

Erin brought the map back to the table and helped herself to a sheet from his notepad. "Maybe they're scrambled up."

"Maybe." Alec bent over the pad and applied several theories, various codes to the letters. Nothing jumped out at him. He sipped his coffee and shook his head. "Nothing. I got nothing. What are you telling me, Lafitte?"

He glanced at Erin's sheet and found her doodling. Filling in the O's and enlarging the dot over the I. He rolled his eyes and returned to his own work. But something about her pad niggled at him.

"*X* marks the spot?" she mumbled.

"Let me see that." He slid her doodle page from under her fingers and studied it, the filled in O's. "Ocom... Dot com." He surged out of his chair and jabbed the power button on his computer. "Maybe it's a website address. A URL."

Erin came to hover behind him, and her sweet vanilla scent teased him. His hands flew across the keyboard, typing in the address. A blank screen popped up, then a prompt for a password to enter the site.

"A password?" Erin moaned. "How are we supposed to know the password?"

"I told you. Daniel and I think alike. The password is something I'll know." He twisted his mouth as he thought. He tried P-I-R-A-T-E first.

Invalid response.

"Hm. Too obvious."

C-O-L-O-M-B-I-A.

"Why Colombia?" Erin asked.

"Last place I saw Daniel. We were on a mission in the Colombian rain forest when—"

Invalid response.

"When?"

He gave her a side glance. "Never mind."

She grunted. "Try *muleheaded*. If Daniel knows you like I do, that's as likely as anything else."

He entered her suggestion to humor her. And gloated when *Invalid response* popped on the screen. He rocked his chair backward and steepled his fingers against his lips as he racked his brain. *Lafitte, Ramirez* and *Blackbeard* received similar results.

"You said Daniel is from Louisiana, right?" she asked, tapping her tooth with a fingernail.

Alec typed in *Louisiana* while she continued thinking aloud. "And the site is 'lil xtra.' Little extra as in—"

"Lagniappe," he finished for her.

"Yeah." She sounded surprised that he knew the term. "The Creole word that means a little something extra, like a special gift."

"Or the name of his hometown." Alec hit the enter key. "Bingo. We're in."

Chapter 6

Before turning his attention to the website, Alec presented Erin with her own lagniappe. A smile.

Not one of his corner-of-the-mouth twitches or his sarcastic grimaces, but a light-the-room, stop-her-heart smile. Erin's breath stuttered from her lungs, and weak-kneed, she dropped onto the chair next to him. Alec's smile transformed the craggy features of his face, softening the hard lines and warming his blue eyes. *Devastating.*

But the all-business facade returned as Alec studied the images on the screen. "What the—? This can't be right."

"What's wrong?" Concern plucked at Erin as a confused glower shaded Alec's face.

"These pictures...the date stamp says April twenty-eighth of this year."

Dragging her attention back to the computer monitor, Erin scrutinized the picture of a Hispanic man stepping out of a black limo. "So?"

"That's Ramirez, the rebel leader Daniel and I were tracking on our last assignment. On April twenty-sixth, two days *before* this picture, we were set to capture him. But all hell broke loose." He sent her hooded glance. "Ramirez was shot by snipers from a rival militia."

A chill settled over Erin, imagining Alec in the midst of such a volatile scenario. Her mouth dried. "Dear God, what did you do?"

"Daniel and I aborted our mission and got out of the area before our cover could be blown." His face darkened. "Or at least *I* got out. Daniel's been missing ever since I gave the order to pull back."

Anguish washed over Alec's face, but he visibly shoved the pain down, firming his jaw and blanking the emotion from his eyes. The pain he denied burrowed to Erin's core and stung her eyes. He could avoid the truth all he wanted, but avoidance didn't change fact. The man grieved for his friend.

And if he could feel that deeply for his work partner, how much more could he love a woman? Erin shivered remembering the leashed passion in his kiss last night, the intensity she saw whenever she looked into his eyes. Beneath all his rigid control and focused energy, she had no doubt Alec Kincaid was a wellspring of complex emotions—whether he chose to address those feelings or not.

He tapped the monitor with a finger. "This date has to be wrong. If Ramirez *wasn't* dead on the twenty-eighth, he should have been close to it. He took at least one head shot. No way he survived. So how—"

"You're sure that's Ramirez in the picture?" Erin narrowed her gaze on the mustachioed man in the photo.

"Yeah." Alec enlarged the picture and zoomed in on the man's neck. "See that mole. Next to it, the line there. That's a scar he got while in prison."

"So it's either him or a really good imposter, huh?"

"It's him." Certainty set the grim slash of Alec's mouth.

"So then the man you saw in the jungle that day. He—"

"Was the imposter." He banged the desk with his fist. "Damn it, I knew something wasn't right with the whole scene. Ramirez always travels with a whole entourage of bodyguards. See here in the photo, all these guys he's got with him?"

"Mmm-hmm." But rather than the picture, Erin studied Alec. His expression reflected the rapid succession of realizations that unfolded in his mind.

"The guy in the jungle that day only had one guard with him. Before I could reason through the anomaly, the shooting started."

"You were watching the wrong man?"

"We were set up." Anger flashed in his dark eyes, and a muscle in his jaw jumped. "Fed phony intel. I'd bet the whole deal, the plane, the meeting in the clearing was all for our benefit. Someone wanted to flush us out, wanted to snare us in a trap."

"The other militia?"

He shook his head. "Doesn't fit. Why storm the clearing and kill the players before Daniel and I showed our hand?"

"So maybe this rival militia caught wind of the same phony intelligence you had and thought they were going to bag the leader of their enemy."

"Maybe. That still doesn't tell me who sold us out."

She studied the fire in his eyes as he analyzed the new information. Energy vibrated from him, and a ripple of sensation rolled through her like a shockwave. Just being near this man, seeing him operate, knowing his mind was as strong as his body, filled her with an awe and respect that pooled low in her belly.

"Daniel knows." The low grate of his voice and the piercing stare he sent her echoed with the same conviction. "That's why he disappeared. He knows who set us up."

Erin swallowed hard. "So why doesn't he just tell you! Why all the hidden messages and obscurity?"

"If I was being followed, stands to reason he had a tail, too. He's lying low, watching his back. He can't just send me the information without risking a leak. He has to stay invisible for some reason."

"No written or electronic record. Plausible deniability. The whole theory behind black ops. Right?"

He hesitated. "That may be true for the bureaucrats. Our reasons for being careful, for leaving no physical trail, are more personal. Lives are at stake if we screw up. Not just our lives. Our informants. Other operatives in the field. Innocents." He reached out and brushed his knuckles along her cheek, and a dizzying tingle raced through her. "People like you who get caught in the crossfire."

Regret softened the hard edge to his jaw, and he cupped her chin in his hand. "I'm sorry for getting you involved in this mess. If there'd been another way to keep you safe…"

The lulling rasp of his voice skimmed over her like a caress, and a warm lethargy flooded her body. Despite the harrowing trip to this hideaway, she felt safer with Alec than she had in years. But how long would he feel compelled to guard her? Once he left, how did she know she and the baby would be out of harm's way?

"When will I be able to go home?"

His mouth tightened as he thought. "As soon as I find out what Daniel knows, find the people behind the fiasco in the jungle."

"The same people who hired Manny and his sidekick, I bet."

His lips quirked sideways, and she longed to see another of his full-fledged smiles.

"You catch on quick." Alec turned back to the computer

and clicked through the series of surveillance photos of Ramirez. "More of the same."

His nimble fingers danced across the keyboard, and she imagined those same deft hands moving over her body, skillfully bringing her pleasure. A shudder of anticipation rippled to her marrow. She sighed and stroked a hand over her growing belly. *As if he'd want anything to do with her and her pregnancy-swollen body...*

"Hello, what's this?"

Alec's voice shook her from her daze. A map of Louisiana glowed from the screen, and he studied the monitor with assessing scrutiny. "Will you bring me the pirate map from the table?"

Erin retrieved the fake parchment and handed it to Alec. The jangle of excitement stirred in her gut, the sense that they were onto something important.

He held the map against the monitor image, and the light from the screen seeped dimly through the paper. The scrawled lines Daniel had drawn in black ink stood out.

"Look." Alec couldn't hide the excitement in his voice. "His marks corresponded perfectly with the highways and country roads between his hometown in the north, southward to this tiny *X* on the map."

"Is he telling you to go to this place he's mapped out?"

"So it would seem." Alec's countenance radiated a hopefulness and assurance. Seeing Alec's morale raised buoyed her own spirits. When she looked closer at the map of Louisiana, she sent Alec a dubious frown. "Correct me if I'm wrong, but isn't that part of Louisiana mostly marshland and bayous? Why would Daniel want you to go into the swamp?"

He refolded Daniel's letter, hit Print to make a hard copy of the Louisiana map, then pinned a penetrating stare on her. "That's what I intend to find out."

* * *

Restless, Alec prowled the main room of the bunker, ex-
amining the new facts of the case from every angle while he
gathered gear and supplies in preparation for leaving.

By contrast, Erin was still and quiet while, with steady
artist's hands, she drew the lines from Daniel's letter on the
Louisiana map. GPS coordinates made her efforts a waste of
time, but the task kept her occupied while he planned their
trip to the alligator-infested swamps of south Louisiana.

He hadn't informed Erin yet that he was taking her with
him. He didn't dare leave her alone, even here in the relative
safety of the bunker. Learning that he and Daniel had likely
been set up that day in the jungle rattled Alec, shook him to
the core. Someone he'd trusted had betrayed him, had nearly
gotten him killed. Until he knew what he was dealing with,
who he was up against, he wanted Erin at his side, where he
knew he could keep her safe.

He paused for a moment from his packing to watch Erin
draw. A loose curl of hair skimmed her cheek, while she
hunched over her work, her slim fingers gracefully sketching.
Admiration tugged in his chest. She'd been a surprising help
to him in the past two days, her insights and instincts sharp
and accurate, her artistic talent commendable. The woman
was both bright and beautiful. A potent combination.

Erin bit her lower lip in concentration, and his senses were
assailed with the memory of sucking that same lip into his
mouth and sampling it with his tongue. Heat spun through
him, remembering her hungry response to his kiss, her sweet
taste. A low growl rumbled from his throat as the desire to
kiss her again swelled like a storm inside him.

Her tempting chocolate eyes angled up from her work with
an exasperated glance. "You're hovering."

Alec gritted his teeth and reined in the tempest brewing
in his blood. Chocolate eyes, vanilla scent and caramel hair.

Damn it, the woman was a sensual feast for a starving man. A sexy sundae he longed to melt with his heat, then lap up each last drop. He envisioned her naked and pliant in his arms while he licked sticky sweetness from her skin....

Holy freakin' moley! His body on fire, Alec rocketed from his chair with a loud huff.

"I'm doing my best!" she protested, misunderstanding the source of his current agitation.

"I'll be back," he muttered as he strode toward the ladder that led out to the cave. "I need air." More accurately, he needed the shock of the icy outdoors to bring him back to his senses and cool the lava in his veins. *I'd bet you've never run from a problem....*

If only she knew.

Alec raced up the rungs, his body taut with tension, and he shouldered open the trapdoor. Escaping. Running. *Coward.*

What was wrong with him? Where was his self-control? The need and desire that pounded through him were overwhelming, staggering. He'd been dangerously close to breaking his promise not to kiss her again, moments away from tossing her across the Murphy bed and sating the raging beast that howled inside him. Oddly, knowing she was pregnant added a sharp-edged twist to the need pulsing through him. He was more protective of her, more determined to defend her and...at the same time, to claim her for himself.

He leaned against the wall of the chilly cave and laughed bitterly as he cast his gaze along the dank rock. He even had the right setting for his caveman mentality.

Get over it, buddy. You've no place in your life for a woman and her kid. Family, loved ones, friends made him vulnerable to the scum that wanted to manipulate him. If he didn't allow himself personal relationships, his enemies couldn't use the people he cared about against him.

Alec huffed out a deep breath that billowed like a silvery

cloud in the icy air. He'd made his choice, had known the isolated and lonely existence he'd lead when he'd joined the world of black ops and counterterrorism. But his work, protecting his country, was worth the price.

Alec wound his way to the mouth of the cave and discovered that snow had piled up overnight and blocked the cave exit.

"Damnation!" Growling his determination, Alec scooped at the snow mound with his hands, digging fruitlessly. He chiseled out a small hole only to find equally high piles of the white stuff blanketing the mountainside. Until the sun had time to work its melting magic, they were snowbound.

Alec punched the ice wall with his fist. He had a fix on Daniel's location, leads to track down, traitors to unearth. But for the foreseeable future he'd be sitting tight, wasting precious time, while cooped up with a sweet temptation his duty and honor dictated he must resist.

"I'm taking you with me to Louisiana," Alec announced over a dinner of canned chili that night.

Erin paused, her spoon halfway to her mouth. "You don't think I'd be safe here alone?"

"I think you'd be safer with me, where I can protect you."

He continued eating, but his comment resonated inside her, stirring a fuzzy warmth. He'd elected himself her personal bodyguard and defender. She smiled. "Your dedication to protecting me is sweet. Very chivalrous."

His eyebrows puckered, and he sent her a dubious frown. "Sweet's got nothing to do with it. Until this is over, you're my responsibility. It's my duty to keep you alive."

"Oh." The glow of romanticism she'd indulged in dimmed. "I guess I thought…never mind."

His spoon clinked in his empty bowl. "Don't take it personally. I like you just fine. But that has nothing to do with anything. My job is to find my partner, figure out who's been sabotaging our work in Colombia and keep you from getting killed in the process. I can't let the lines get blurred, or I'll lose perspective and professional objectivity."

A hollow sensation plucked at her. She understood his reasoning, the necessity for his distance. Yet in the past few days, she'd come to admire so much about Alec. She'd hoped he felt a mutual respect for her. And their kiss…

She pressed her lips together when they tingled with the memory of his ardor and skill. Had she been the only one who'd felt the promise in that kiss? She knew what Alec had said last night about not kissing her again, but she'd also seen the way he looked at her as they worked on the map this morning. The heat in his eyes was unmistakable.

With a frustrated grunt, he pushed to his feet and stormed from the table. He'd been tightly wound in the hours since he'd discovered the snow had trapped them, delaying their departure.

Erin rubbed a hand over the bump at her belly and broached a topic that had been nagging her for the last two days. "Alec, how are we supposed to get back to civilization? We have no car, no plane and no bridge, thanks to your precaution of cutting the ropes."

He shifted his deep blue gaze toward her for a moment, but said nothing. His expression gave nothing away.

"Alec?"

"I'll send word to a contact of mine when we're ready to be airlifted out. There's a place a few miles from here where a chopper can land."

"So we hike down to this landing spot? What about that big gulch out there? How are we supposed to get back across?" She noticed a slight movement in his face, almost a wince. Suspicion and alarm wrenched her stomach. "Alec?"

"We won't go across." He swallowed hard and faced her with his jaw firmly set. "We'll go down it. Rappelling."

Erin clapped a hand to her mouth as the contents of her stomach lurched. A cold, sinking dread crashed down on her, and she moaned.

The last time she'd been rappelling, she'd watched Bradley die.

Chapter 7

Alec had expected the notion of rappelling wouldn't sit well with Erin, but he'd never imagined she'd react as drastically as she did.

Her face paled. Her hands shook. Tears blossomed in her wide, dark eyes.

He raised a hand, ready to counter her arguments. "I know you think you can't do it. But I'll walk you through every step. I swear I won't let anything hap—"

"No!" She stood and stumbled back from the table so fast, her chair toppled with a crash. "Please, don't—" With a hiccupping gulp, a keening moan tore from her throat, a terrifying sound that scraped down Alec's spine and raised the hairs at his nape.

"Erin?" As he stepped around the counter, not sure how he could calm her, she wrapped an arm around her middle and doubled over. Alec rushed forward and caught her before she slumped to the floor.

Panic slammed through him, an unfamiliar feeling for a

man trained to keep a cool head in the direst of situations. "Erin! What's wrong? Is it the baby?"

"B-Bradley…" she rasped, flinging her arms around Alec's neck and clinging to him. Her whole body shook, and sobs racked her chest.

"What about Bradley, sweetcakes?"

"Dead… H-he fell!" she stuttered through her tears. "I c-couldn't help him. An a-anchor failed, and h-his rope… He—"

Understanding dawned, yanking a knot in his gut. "Bradley died while rappelling?"

Her head bobbed, and a fresh gush of tears trickled down her cheeks. "I s-saw it all. I couldn't h-help him. I… Alec, it was awful! He—"

"Shh." He touched a finger to her lips, his heart aching for the horror she'd witnessed. He'd seen people die, but never someone he loved. He could hardly imagine the agony she'd suffered.

Scooping her limp form into his arms, Alec held her close, carried her to the sofa and sat down with her in his lap. He was at a loss how to ease her pain, and that sense of helplessness rankled, leaving him even more off balance. A choice curse word formed in his mind, but he swallowed it. Here was another reason to avoid emotional entanglements. This useless, clawing sympathy sucked.

"Please, Alec…" She sniffed and angled wet, red eyes up to him. "I can't do it. I'm afraid I-I'll freeze or… I don't know. I just c-can't…"

"Aw, sweetcakes…" He swiped a thumb under her eye, drying her tears, then smoothed a hand down her silky curls. For several minutes he simply held her, his arms wrapped securely around her trembling body as if he could absorb the shock, the misery, and take away her pain.

As her sobs receded and her tremors eased, he grew

sharply aware of how good she felt crushed against his chest, held snugly in his embrace with her round bottom perched on his lap. Drawing deep breaths to rein in his libido only filled his lungs with her sweet womanly essence, her tempting vanilla scent.

Erin nestled her face in the curve of his neck, and the tickle of her hair under his chin, on his cheek, teased him and sensitized his skin.

"Please…don't make me do it, Alec," she murmured, her breath hot against his throat.

"I know you'll be scared. I understand that. But we have to—"

Her grip tightening, she lifted wide eyes and shook her head. "No! Please. There has to be another way out of here."

Her plea mingled with the pulse of desire rising inside him, tangling with his frustrating inability to comfort her, morphing into an aching need far stronger than mere lust. He could no longer separate the clambering impulse to kiss her from his steely determination to protect her.

"Please, Alec…" When she met his eyes, his breath lodged in his throat. His heart rolled in his chest. Determination besieged him to do whatever was necessary to allay Erin's fears and to protect her from the pain of her loss.

He finger-combed tear-dampened wisps of hair away from her face and pressed a kiss to her forehead. "Okay. I'll find another way down from here."

"Really?"

The relief and gratitude that welled in her eyes humbled him. He'd never savored a greater sense of victory or accomplishment, even after completing a tedious mission.

A thin smile tugged the corners of her mouth, though her bottom lip still quivered. She cupped a hand against his cheek and whispered, "Thank you."

He covered her hand with his. Laced their fingers. Kissed her palm.

Erin sucked in a sharp breath and dropped her gaze to the spot he'd kissed, then to his lips. He felt the tremor that raced through her, watched her pupils dilate and her cheeks flush.

His own breath hissed through his teeth as she leaned in, lifting her mouth toward his. A siren in the back of his mind screamed a warning that this was wrong, that his honor demanded he not take advantage of her vulnerability.

But her lips touched his before sanity could pull him back, and he was lost.

She nibbled his bottom lip tentatively at first, testing. The tiny kisses sizzled through his blood like sparks eating up a fuse, inching toward a powder keg. Tensing, he tapped every ounce of his restraint not to seize control of the kiss and ravage her mouth.

With a mewling sigh, she angled her head and captured his lips fully. She slid her hands up, spearing her fingers into his hair to cradle his head and tug him nearer.

His body thrummed, and his head felt muzzy. He drew on her lips, imbibing the sweetness she offered. When her tongue made a foray into his mouth, he greeted her boldness with a throaty growl of approval. Meeting her parry, he engaged her in an erotic duel.

He hadn't kissed another woman in a long time, but he couldn't remember the taste of a woman's lips or the gentle pressure of a woman's mouth ever filling his senses like Erin's did. Her kiss made him shake with need and longing. She touched a place deep into his soul and wrenched feelings from him he'd never experienced before.

She scared the hell out of him.

Drawing on the last thread of his willpower, Alec pulled away from her and dragged in a ragged breath. As much as he wanted to push her down on the sofa and make love to her, a louder voice in his head reminded him of his duty to protect her. Even from himself.

He couldn't, he *wouldn't* take advantage of her need for comfort and manipulate it for his own pleasure. Scooting her legs off his lap, he shoved away from the sofa.

"Alec?"

He heard the hurt and confusion in her voice and gritted his teeth. A strangling tightness squeezed his chest, made him want to run back to her and promise her anything, just to soothe the pain his rejection caused her. But he didn't have the luxury of making her promises, of giving her anything other than his protection—at least as long as the threat Daniel had uncovered hung over their heads.

"I need to study a map of the area, find a route we can hike down." He stalked to the wall near the computer, where a topographical map was tacked up, and yanked it down.

He spread the map on the computer desk and dragged a hand down his cheek. The taste of Erin's kiss lingered, taunting him as he scanned the elevation and directional markings. Their best move, it seemed, was to head north, then hike down from the far side of the mountain.

His smartest course of action was to keep his rampaging testosterone in check and leave Erin the hell alone. He'd kept plenty of femmes fatales at a distance, stayed emotionally unencumbered and kept his fly zipped countless times in the past. So why did Erin weaken his defenses and rattle his control?

She rose from the sofa and chafed her arms. "I'm sorry. I know you must think I'm a real wimp. I mean the way I freaked out about rappelling… I—"

"You have a right to be freaked by it. You witnessed something no one should have to see. I understand." He sensed more than saw her step up beside him to look over his shoulder at the map.

"The ironic thing is I used to do so many things with Bradley. Surfing, parasailing, rock climbing, skydiving…" She sighed and dropped into Daniel's computer chair. "And, well…other stuff. Bradley couldn't wait to push the boundaries and take his adventures, as he called them, to the next level."

Her confession startled him. He hadn't expected this daring side of Erin. She'd seemed so intimidated by the paces he'd put her through getting up to the bunker. But her memories of Bradley's tragic death explained her current fear of such daredevil endeavors. "So you and Bradley were both adrenaline junkies, huh?"

She grunted. "He was. I'd have been happy just camping out or walking nature trails in national parks. I had to do a bit of soul searching to work up the nerve to jump out of a plane with him. Shooting a class-four rapid in a kayak and bungee jumping were a little scary, too."

He peered up at her from the map. "You went bungee jumping?"

"Uh-huh. Nothing too high up, though. And Bradley really had to lay the guilt trip on hard to get me up there." A sad smile ghosted over her lips, a wistfulness that unsettled Alec. "But I did it. Because I didn't want to let him down. Didn't want to be left behind."

Erin stared down at her hands in her lap, her eyebrows furrowed.

Alec pushed the map aside and studied her slumped shoulders, uneasy with the direction of the conversation. "Bradley made you feel guilty if you didn't do all these stunts with him?"

She shrugged. "Sort of. He'd…challenge me." She peeked up briefly, then lowered her gaze again. "He wouldn't let me give in to my fears and back out. He'd say, 'Where's your sense of adventure, Erin? You aren't going to chicken out after we've come this far, are you?'" She gave a quiet, nervous-sounding laugh, and she squeezed her hands into fists in her lap.

Alec read her body language, listened to the warbling tone of her voice and filled in the blanks. The urge to wrap his hands around Bradley's neck shot through him like a bullet burning a path through his soul.

Erin scrunched her nose and glanced at him. "And he had this look. His eyes would get all sad like he was disappointed in me, and without saying a word, he'd have me doing things I never would have dreamed I'd do."

Fury boiled through Alec's blood, but he forcibly shoved it down to keep his voice neutral. "He manipulated you."

Erin's head snapped up. "No!"

"That's what it sounds like to me. He sounds like a self-serving bastard who didn't care how you felt and who coerced you to follow him on his adrenaline trips by making you feel like less of a person for your reluctance. He took your love for him and your desire to make him happy and used it against you."

Horror and hurt blazed in Erin's eyes, and for a moment she only gaped at him. Finally she drew her shoulders back and pulled in a deep breath. "You're wrong. Bradley was a good man. He loved me. He just wanted me to push myself, to experience life to the fullest."

"His idea of a full life or yours?" He'd said too much, crossed the line. He knew that, yet his disgust with Bradley goaded him on. "You said yourself you always wanted children, wanted to raise a family with him. *That* was your dream. So how full is your life now as a widow, facing motherhood alone?"

Erin gasped, lurched to her feet. "That's a horrible thing to say!"

The pain and anger in her eyes castigated him. He drew

a slow breath to keep his tone even. "I just think that if he cared about you, he'd have respected your needs, your feelings, your dreams."

She blinked slowly, and a tear escaped her thick fringe of eyelashes. That lone tear sent a sucker punch to his gut. He had no right to make judgments and less right to voice them, to cast aspersions on the man she'd married, no matter what he thought of her choice. So why had he pushed? Why had he felt compelled to shake up her memories of her husband?

Alec kneaded the back of his neck and puffed out a harsh sigh. "Damn it, Erin. I'm sorry. I shouldn't have—"

He shoved to his feet and stalked to the kitchen. Somewhere in the cabinets, surely he or Daniel had stashed a bottle of bourbon or rum or *something*. Anything with a bite to it.

As he ransacked the shelves, Erin moved into his peripheral vision and pressed a hand over her belly. Concerned, he gave her a more thorough scrutiny and noticed her wan complexion.

"Are you all right? Do you feel sick again?" He grabbed out a box of crackers from the cabinet. "Do you need to eat?"

"When Bradley died," she said, her voice almost a whisper, "I was so mad at him. I was hurt and sad and numb with grief, too, but mostly I was mad."

Alec swallowed hard as his chest contracted. He set the box of crackers on the counter and let her talk. He'd said his piece, and now he owed it to her to listen, as difficult as it might be to hear about her heartache and turmoil.

"After all I'd done so he wouldn't leave me behind...he left me anyway. He died, and I was all alone. But as angry as I was with him, I was more furious with myself."

"Yourself? Why?" Alec took a step toward her, wanting to touch her, to hold her, but knowing he didn't have any right.

"He was coming to help me...when he fell. My line had gotten hung up somehow, and when he tried to come help me...one of his anchors failed and—" A shiver shook her, and she hugged herself. "It was my f-fault."

Alec mumbled a curse under his breath and wrapped her in his arms. "It's not your fault."

"That's easy to say. Not so easy to believe. Especially considering what happened with Joey Finley."

Alec wrinkled his brow. "With who?"

She shook her head, wiggled free of his arms. "Forget it. I've dumped enough on you."

Erin dashed the moisture from her cheeks and squared her shoulders. "I'm tired. I think I'll take a nap."

Clamping down on the painful whirlwind filling in his chest, he nodded. He watched her crawl under the covers of the Murphy bed and pull the sheets up to her chin.

How the hell had she managed to burrow under his skin and free all the emotions he'd kept locked away for years? Caring for Erin, feeling so much for her, was dangerous. To him. To her. The woman had suffered enough. He refused to add to her pain, and he knew he could offer her nothing but more heartbreak. He had to squelch his obsession with her and get himself under control before his unwise attraction to her burned them both.

Before his distraction got them both killed.

Erin rested for the next hour, but her thoughts wouldn't let her sleep. Alec's opinion of Bradley stung, partly because he'd voiced a belief that had been lurking at the back of her mind. She wouldn't have even been on that mountain rappelling if Bradley had respected her reluctance to climb down that cliff. Yet how could she resent Bradley's high-pressure tactics when he'd died trying to save her?

Erin rolled over and punched the pillow as her thoughts took another pendulum swing. Bradley's death had underscored a different sort of phobia from the one that paralyzed her while rappelling. A fear, rooted in her childhood, still thrived inside her and gnawed her gut in moments like this. Life was so fragile, so unpredictable and so prone to steal one's dreams and the people she loved. Tragedy had left her alone and empty-handed more than once. Was it selfish and weak to just want a quiet, secure life holding the people she loved close to her?

After losing first her parents and then Bradley, Joey's death had shaken her life. She'd retreated from life to her lick her wounds, giving up a career she loved while she grieved and mustered the nerve to face an uncertain future. Only in the past few months had she decided what she wanted and set a course toward rebuilding her life.

Then Alec came along and rattled her safe, well-planned existence. Suddenly she was back in a world of chaos and danger, at risk of losing the security and peace she wanted for herself and her child.

The low rumble of his voice as he placed a phone call to arrange their pickup with someone from his black ops team drew her attention. *Black ops,* she thought, and shivered. The stark contrast between her life and Alec's shouldn't have bothered her so much. But it did. The man who'd comforted her, soothed her when the memory of Bradley's death had overwhelmed her hormone-laden and taxed system, didn't mesh in her mind with a man who hunted terrorists.

I'll find another way down from here.

His concession to her fear, his willingness to inconvenience himself in order to comfort her, surprised her. Pleasantly so. She couldn't remember the last time someone had put her needs and wishes first. His kindness settled in her soul like a warm blanket on a cold night. Comforting, reassuring, safe. Not words she'd have associated with Alec when she'd first met him. Not traits he likely saw in himself.

Yet earlier, Alec had been so sweet and gentle, she'd let

herself take refuge in the solace he offered. She'd sunk into the lulling murmur of his deep voice and drowned in the oblivion of his kiss. A shiver chased over her skin. Dear heaven, the man could curl her toes with his kiss....

Alec ended his call and glanced her way. When she met his gaze, his brow puckered in a frown. "I'm sorry. Did I wake you?"

"No. Couldn't sleep. Too many things on my mind."

"Well, if one of those things is us getting off the mountain, put it out of your head. I've got a plan that involves a minimum of risk or daring on your part."

Erin sat up on the bed and wrapped her arms around her bent knees. "So I heard. We're hiking out and meeting a helicopter, huh?"

He nodded. "It won't be an easy hike, even if most of it is downhill. But there'll be no parachuting, no rappelling, no rope bridges—"

Erin nodded and smiled her appreciation. "And I promise to keep myself pulled together for the duration. No more tears, no more falling apart."

Silently Erin prayed fate didn't toss anything more trying than a snowy hike and a helicopter ride in her path to test her resolve. But fate hadn't been particularly kind to her in the past.

Chapter 8

"Why did you bring me with you?" Erin asked the next morning as they bundled up in preparation to hike down the mountain. "You could have left me in a hotel, left me at the hospital, left me with Knife and his pal. But you didn't."

Alec scoffed as if the answer were obvious, when, in fact, he'd been asking himself the same question since the moment he'd returned to her house to rescue her from William Manny's knife. "They would have killed you."

"Maybe so. It still would have been a lot easier for you to leave me when you had the chance."

He continued filling his pack with accessories for camping that night and navigating the snowy mountain. "No one has ever accused me of doing things the easy way."

"But I'd bet you don't purposely make things harder on yourself, either. I had to have made things harder for you this week."

Harder? Oh, yeah, he'd spent a great deal of the past days hard. He gritted his teeth against the flash of heat her unintended double entendre called to his mind.

When she moved up beside him and touched his arm, he resisted the urge to flinch away from her searing touch. Memories of their ill-advised kisses and what could easily have happened yesterday on the couch scorched his brain.

"I just want to understand why you'd do this for me when you didn't have to."

He met the shadows of doubt darkening her chocolate eyes. Her uncertainty spoke for just how little she'd had anyone looking out for her interests in the past. Her late husband's selfishness galled him. If she were *his* wife…

Alec caught his breath, stopped the thought before it fully formed. He had no business thinking of Erin in any context other than an innocent woman who needed him to return her safely home so she could get on with her life. That meant nixing the threat that hung over her because of his mistakes.

Alec rolled the tension from his shoulders. "I don't know why."

She opened her mouth to probe the issue further, and he cut her off, eager to change the subject. "Hand me the emergency heat packs over there on the counter, will you?"

Her grave expression as she handed him the chemical packs that could mean the difference between hypothermia and survival told him she understood their hike was still filled with inherent dangers. But she didn't complain, didn't protest.

With Erin's help, he had the bunker secured within the hour, and they headed up the ladder into the biting winter wind.

"We want to move fast, get to the pickup spot as quickly as possible so we can make camp and build a fire before nightfall," Alec said as he adjusted one of the packs on her shoulders. "But you need to watch out for ice on the rocks. It will be steep in places, and the winds will be tricky on the north side of the mountain."

"Got it." She gave him a confident nod.

"Stay close. Tell me if you need a break to rest."

"I'll be fine. Lead on, Captain." She flashed another grin that made him hate the idea of telling her goodbye when they reached civilization.

But if he'd gotten correct information from Jake, their pilot, when he arranged for the helicopter to meet them, the crashed and burned-out plane had led authorities to pronounce Alec dead. Just as he'd hoped. Now only select few members of his black ops team knew he was alive and where to find him.

Erin was safe to go home. She could finish preparations for welcoming her baby to the world. A pang wrenched through him when he thought of Erin bringing her child home from the hospital alone, facing parenting by herself.

From nowhere, a startling image flickered in his mind of himself at her side, playing the father role and sharing in the baby's homecoming. He gave his head a brisk shake. Clearly the past few days cooped up with her had toyed with his wiring. He was the last person who needed to set up house and try to be a father.

What did he know about home and hearth and all things domestic? He certainly had no reference point from his own youth. When he'd joined the black ops team, he'd sacrificed any notions of home and family to his job.

Alec hoisted his backpack to his shoulders, then led the way down toward the far side of the mountain. As he hiked, battered by the icy wind, his thoughts turned to his future with the black ops team once he found Daniel and rooted out the traitor among them.

"Do you think Daniel is at this location in Louisiana he mapped out? Do you think that's why he sent the letter?" Erin's question drew him out of his deliberations. Clearly her thoughts ran along lines similar to his.

"Maybe. More likely he's pointing me toward information about who sold us out. Covering his bases in case—" Alec blamed the blast of cold wind for stealing his breath and causing the strangling tightness in his chest.

"In case?" Erin prompted quietly.

Alec redistributed the weight of his backpack on his shoulders and squelched the thought of losing his partner. "In case something happens to him. He wants me to bring the scum responsible for betraying us to justice."

Every man for himself. Don't jeopardize the mission. Alec reminded himself he had no reason to feel guilty. And yet...

"You picked any names for your baby?" He couldn't be sure where the question came from, but he grasped at anything to get his mind off his missing partner. Off his recent string of costly mistakes—letting Manny and his partner escape, kissing Erin, letting her under his skin.

"A few," Erin said, already sounding winded from their hike. "If it's a girl, she'll be Annie. For my mother."

He stepped carefully over a fallen and icy tree in the path and turned to help her step over the obstacle. "I like it. What if it's a boy?"

"Hmm. I could go a number of ways there. *Bradley* would be an obvious choice."

Acid burned his gut. He swung back around and crunched through the snow without telling her what he thought of that name. He assured himself his dislike for Erin's late husband had to do with the man's manipulation of Erin's feelings and not envy over her continued loyalty to the father of her child.

The bite of acid grew hollow and cold as he marched on through the frozen woods. Other than Daniel, Alec couldn't remember anyone ever showing him such undying faith and commitment. Certainly not his mother. He'd been looking out for himself most of his life.

"Maybe *Howard,* for my dad." Erin's chipper tone pulled him from the dark track of his thoughts. She chuckled. "But

Howard Bauer is kind of a tongue twister. I couldn't do that to my child."

He forced a grin. "Your child thanks you."

When she grew quiet, Alec knew without looking her hand had slipped to her belly to stroke the growing swell. Erin wouldn't be the sort of mother who left her son to fend for himself on the streets. Gritting his teeth, he shoved down the morose track of his thoughts.

"I've thought about the name Joey, too. But…I don't know. Maybe not."

"Why *Joey?*"

She didn't answer right away, and he slowed his pace enough to glance back at her, check that she was all right.

Her head was down her, her brow puckered, hinting at the deep, upsetting path of her thoughts. Then he remembered her mentioning someone named Joey Finley before. Remembered her troubled reaction to the name.

"Will you tell me about Joey Finley?" he asked, pitching his voice low.

"I…" She hesitated. Sighed. "That's a rather fresh wound. Talking about it is like ripping off a bandage, making it bleed again. And since I promised to keep a stiff upper lip for the duration…" She attempted a teasing grin that fell short of its mark.

"I only asked because you've mentioned him before." He shook his head and picked up his pace. "You don't have to tell me if it hurts too much. I understand."

Silence fell between them for several steps, and Alec focused on the terrain ahead. The mountain dropped off sharply and hiking the steeper incline would be harder and more treacherous.

"They say wounds heal better given air," Erin said a moment later, and he heard the reluctance in her voice.

"You don't have to talk about it—"

"It's okay. I probably should. It's just…"

The crunch of her footsteps stopped, and he pivoted to find her looking out at the white-capped mountain range. She hunched deeper into the large parka she'd borrowed from him. When she spoke, a frosty cloud formed from her breath. "Joey was one of my students, a first-grader. He was a precious little boy, but smaller than the rest of the kids in his class. Kind of a loner."

She angled a melancholy glance toward him that drilled into his chest and dredged up buried memories of his own childhood.

"I took a special interest in him, because he seemed to be having such a hard time. The other boys weren't mean to him exactly, but they didn't include him, either. Joey's self-confidence was pretty low, and I just wanted him to know he had a friend, wanted him to not give up on himself. To keep believing in himself. I never—" The color leached from her face, and she hugged herself tighter.

Alec tensed, too, sensing the emotional blow creeping up on him, waiting to attack. "Erin, don't do this if it upsets—"

"He was dyslexic, it turns out." She gave a sad smile and plowed on with her story. "That's why he was having so much trouble learning to write his name."

When her voice cracked, she drew a deep breath. Erin composed herself and leveled her shoulders before she continued. She forged on with grit and courage and determination, despite the ominous shadows lurking in her eyes. "One day he seemed especially upset, so I kept him in from recess to talk with him. To help him. I…told him about going skydiving with Bradley. I told him I'd thought I could never do it, but I did. I told him how many times I had to jump off the platform at the airfield and practice my landing roll before I got the nerve to go up in the airplane. 'If I can jump out of an airplane,' I said, 'then you can write your name. It just takes practice and faith. But I believe in you, Joey. You can do it.'"

Erin's voice quivered, but her eyes stayed dry.

Thank God. Alec wasn't sure he could handle tears right now. He was having a hard enough time hearing her story about a boy who sounded too much like himself. Except he'd never had a teacher take the personal interest in him that Erin had for this child.

Alec cleared the thickness from his throat. "Joey was lucky to have a teacher like you." *Someone who cared.*

Her head whipped around. "Was he?" The bitter note in her voice surprised him. "His parents wouldn't agree. Not after Joey jumped off the third-floor balcony of their apartment trying to be like Ms. Bauer." Her eyes grew bright with emotion, and her voice held a sharp edge.

Dread jerked a knot in Alec's gut. "He died."

"Yes, he died! He thought if his teacher could skydive from an airplane, then he could jump from three floors up with a sheet for a parachute! He broke his neck. Never wrote his name again. Because of me. Because I offered myself as some glowing example of overcoming obstacles and persevering." She slapped a hand against her chest for emphasis. "I only wanted to motivate him, to encourage him. Instead I led him into disaster. I planted the idea in his head that taking risks was something to be admired. I was the worst kind of role model for that child, and he died because of my mistake."

The agony and anguish, the guilt in Erin's voice made Alec's stomach pitch. "Erin, you can't blame yourself—"

"Why not? It *was* my fault! His parents threatened to sue the school if I wasn't fired. Not that I could stay at the school after that anyway. I was heartsick about Joey's death. What kind of teacher gives a child even the *suggestion* that jumping out of a plane is something to brag about? How could I have been so stupid?"

She spun away, trembling, then rubbed her hands over her face. "Damn it, I promised not to fall apart again." She sucked in a deep breath and released a tremulous sigh. "If I could be that careless, that irresponsible as a teacher, I shudder to think what kind of parent I'm going to be." She scoffed. "What was I thinking?"

Alec stepped toward her, squeezed her arm through the thick padding of the parka. "Don't beat yourself up like this."

She shrugged away from his grip and marched on through the snow. "Stop. I deserve a lot worse than beating myself up. That boy *died* because of me."

Alec fell into step beside her. "And where were Joey's parents when he climbed out on that balcony to jump? What about their responsibility?"

She shook her head, walking faster, her steps clipped and angry. He seized her arm again and brought her to an abrupt halt. Turning her toward him, he caught her chin in his fingers. "You may have made a miscalculation when you encouraged that boy, Erin, but you gave him more than some children ever get at home or at school. You shared part of yourself. You cared."

Painful memories seeped out of the dark corners of his soul where he'd locked them. He gritted his teeth so hard his jaw hurt, and he struggled to shove the memories back down. "Don't ever undersell the difference that can make."

She closed her eyes, sighed. When she lifted her gaze to him again, a sad resignation filled her eyes. "I miss my students. I want to teach again, but I'm scared. I don't want to screw up and hurt one of those precious babies."

He tugged her close and tucked her head under his chin. "Don't hide your heart away, Erin. The world needs more teachers like you. Your caring and commitment make all the difference."

Alec released her and stepped back before he did something foolish. Like kiss her. Which he wanted to do so badly his bones ached. Erin's sweetness, her deep love and compassion, was everything he'd been denied growing up. And exactly what he couldn't afford in his line of work.

No matter how the barren part of his soul longed for the love she had to offer, he couldn't give in to the empty ache. Lonely as it was, his position on the black ops team required he maintain the kind of cool dispassion and detachment that had marked his formative years.

He'd be wise to remember that and keep an emotional distance with Erin, as well. She was rapidly becoming far too important to him.

Your caring and commitment make all the difference.

Erin rolled Alec's words around in her mind as she trudged down the path, stepping in the footprints Alec left in the snow. She knew sooner or later she'd have to suck it up and go back to teaching, despite her qualms and the queasy feeling in her stomach when she thought of Joey. Sharing her pain with Alec and receiving his vote of confidence shifted so much inside her. Alec's faith in her buoyed her spirit in a way she hadn't known in years.

By contrast, Bradley's version of inspiration tended toward guilt and manipulation, a thought more sobering than the chilly mountain wind.

"We're getting close now," Alec said, interrupting her thoughts. "Hear that water?"

Erin perked her ears to the swoosh of flowing water. "Yeah. Is that a waterfall?"

"It's a stream at the bottom of this hill. Our pickup point is about a mile past the creek."

She checked her watch. "We made good time then. It's still an hour or more before dark."

He nodded and glanced back at her. "Yeah. You should be

proud of yourself. You've kept up even when I pushed hard. This wasn't easy hiking."

She grinned. "I may be a chicken, but I'm a fit chicken. Is that what you mean?"

He chuckled. "You said it, not me."

At the bottom of the slope, they found the wide stream, splashing along its rocky bed, flowing swiftly down the mountain. In the summer, wading across the thigh-high stream with its strong current and slippery footing would be tricky, but not impossible. Now, however, patches of ice coated the boulders that jutted from the water and glistened on the creek's banks. The sparkling ice testified to the stream's frigid temperature.

Alec braced his hands on his hips and cast his gaze downstream then up.

Erin used the break to catch her breath and study the situation, as well. "How are we going to get across? The water has to be freezing. We'll get hypothermia if we wade."

"Roger that."

Alec led her several hundred yards up the bank of the fast-flowing stream before he stopped and nodded to the rocks. "This looks doable. What do you think? Can you maneuver these gaps?"

He was asking her what she thought? Alec's consideration of her needs created a feeling of fullness in her chest, fluttery and sweet. She appreciated more than she could express his willingness to include her in the decision-making process, taking into account her needs, her abilities, her opinions. Bradley had always decided matters and left it to her to follow or be left behind. Erin eyed the placement of the boulders, the distance between them, and nodded. "I can do it."

"Okay," Alec said, "I'll go first and find the best path. Leave your pack. I'll come back and get it, but I want you to have good balance." He stepped up on the nearest rock and reached down to help her. After dropping her backpack in a patch of dry leaves, she gave him her hand. His firm grip filled her with a reassurance and warmth that radiated throughout her body.

"Watch your footing. Take it slow. There's ice, and the wet algae makes the rocks slippery."

"Gotcha."

Alec turned and leaped to the next boulder. She inched to the edge of the first rock and waited for him to move on before following.

She jumped. Landed smoothly. And breathed a sigh of relief.

As she followed him to the next flat stepping stone, she smiled to herself, remembering leapfrogging rock to rock in the creek that ran behind her house as a child. She'd had pretty good balance as a kid, but occasionally came home with wet shoes. Her mother would roll her eyes and put Erin's shoes by the heater vent to dry.

"Careful, that one's loose."

Alec's voice called her from her memories.

"Okay." She jumped to the rock in question and braced as the stone shifted. Tottering, she used the forward momentum, exaggerated by the wobbling rock, to leap for the next landing. But Alec still surveyed the best route from that stone, and as she landed, she came up short to avoid crashing into him. And her foot slipped.

With a gasp, she grabbed a flap of Alec's backpack to catch herself. She managed to find her balance, barely. But the sudden, unexpected tug at his back, just as he was preparing to jump to the next boulder, threw Alec off.

He circled his arms, teetered. Erin tried to grab for him,

but his foot hit a patch of ice. Her grasp on his shirttail wasn't enough to keep him out of the water. "Alec!"

As he stumbled into the stream, the rushing current sucked him under the swift water.

Chapter 9

Erin's breath snagged in her throat as she watched Alec sink into the icy stream. A frozen heartbeat later, he broke the surface and swiped the frigid water from his face. He let fly a curse that voiced the agonizing discomfort of the wintry stream.

Panic squeezed her chest. "Oh, God!"

This was her fault. *Her fault.* Self-recrimination echoed through her brain as she watched Alec scramble to find his footing. He dragged his pack from his back and heaved it onto the far bank. With his wet clothes plastered to him, he slogged through the water and staggered out. He dropped to his knees, then started peeling off layers of soaked clothing.

Her stomach knotting with guilt, Erin picked her way across the rest of the rocks and rushed to his side.

"Alec! Oh, God, Alec, I'm so sorry!" she moaned as she helped him strip off his wet shirts.

"F-fire. Gotta build-d a f-fire." He shivered so hard in the cold air that his teeth chattered.

"Right. A fire." She jumped up to find whatever dry wood

she could scrounge. She dumped the sticks and stray limbs in a haphazard pile and looked at Alec's soaked pack. Chances were slim any matches in his pack were still dry.

She scrambled back to help him tug his wet jeans and thermal underwear down his hips. When she noticed how much trouble he had unlacing his boots, she took over the job for him. After she yanked the boots off his feet, she finished pulling the jeans down his legs. By now the skin of his legs had grown pale with bluish tones that scared the hell out of her. "Are there any matches or a lighter in my pack?"

Shivering hard, he glanced up at her. She fully expected to find wrath and blame in his eyes, but the helplessness and obvious suffering she saw instead frightened her far more.

"Y-yes-s-s." His lips were white, and his face a raw-looking red.

Her heart lurched, and bile rose in her throat. She blinked back the sting of useless, self-indulgent tears and rallied her composure, focused herself on one goal. Warming Alec. Saving his life.

Stripping off the coat he'd given her that morning, she wrapped it around him. Once she'd pulled off his wet socks, she removed her own shoes to give him her bulky socks, as well. After chafing as much heat as she could into his fingers and cheeks, she wrapped his hands with one of her shirts and his head with another. He looked like a pitiful excuse for a mummy, but it was the best she had until she retrieved the second pack.

"I'll be right back." She couldn't be sure if the bobbing of his head was a nod of understanding or another shudder, but she didn't linger to decide. With as much haste as she dared, Erin retraced her steps across the large rocks to the other side of the stream, grabbed up the backpack and returned. Her own hands numb with cold, she dug in the pack in search of the promised matches. In addition to the matches, she found the chemical heat packs and pulled out as many as she could find.

Her hands shook as she cracked the plastic packets and crushed them between her hands, stirring the ingredients and starting the chemical reaction that emitted low levels of heat.

"Here, hold this." She pressed one pack between Alec's hands and shoved one in each of his socks, hoping to stave of frostbite in his extremities. She prepared one of the larger heat packs for him to hold against his chest under the parka. The packs would help but weren't nearly enough.

Struggling not to lose her composure as Alec shivered harder and harder, she turned her attention to building a fire. A stiff mountain breeze not only made building the fire more difficult, but also more essential. The windchill factor was a dangerous enemy for Alec.

She finally got a small flame started and helped him scoot nearer to the inadequate heat source.

Jerking more dry clothes from her backpack, Erin shoved the parka aside and surveyed the remnants of his wet garments.

"These have to go. You have to get dry." She surprised herself with the authoritative timbre of her voice. When she met his gaze again, she knew the nod this time was permission to forsake modesty. She worked quickly, ridding Alec of his briefs and undershirt and re-dressing him as best she could. His near-convulsive tremors and icy skin were all the sobering reality she needed to distract her from the gorgeous male body she revealed. Rubbed to warm. Touched as she clothed him.

The damp wood and blustery breeze made the tiny fire flicker and dance. She doubted she could get a big enough blaze going to do him any real good. She'd have to trap what heat she could from the chemical packs and her own body to pour life back into Alec. For that, they needed shelter, protection from the wind.

She had experience with tents from her camping days with Bradley, so she snatched the tightly rolled shelter from Alec's backpack and got to work. Despite the wind that fought her efforts, Erin managed to secure the spikes and raise the poles of the two-man dome tent in record time.

Having surrendered the coat and many of her clothes to Alec, Erin was shivering herself by the time she helped him crawl into the shelter. Taking the parka back from Alec, she spread it on the floor for added protection from the frozen earth. She unrolled the one dry sleeping bag, stripped Alec back down to his underwear and helped him inside the bedding.

Darkness was falling outside by the time she bared herself down to her bra and panties and scrunched into the sleeping bag beside him. After cracking the last of the emergency heat packs and stuffing them into their bedding, she zipped their cocoon all the way up and pulled the cover over their heads.

In the dark confines of the sleeping bag, she heard Alec's tremulous breathing, felt the tickle of his crisp body hair and the stark cold of his skin. Though her movement was restricted in the narrow sleeping bag, Erin stroked as much of Alec's body as she could reach. Her sock-clad feet rubbed his calves. Her hands chafed his arms and back, and she cuddled as close to his lean torso as the small mound of her belly would allow.

Finally, weak from exhaustion and sick with fear, she awkwardly draped her limbs around him. Clinging to his trembling body, she closed her eyes. In the silent darkness, she whispered a prayer, bargaining with higher powers, offering her life if Alec's would be spared. A nauseating twist of remorse and culpability slithered through her and settled in her gut.

"I'm sorry. I'm so sorry," she whispered again and again. Finally sleep stole over her and carried her into restless dreams of bitter winds, icy water and dark regrets.

Light filtered in through a gap in the covers over Erin's head, and she blinked at the bright assault on her eyes. She struggled to shake the cobwebs of sleep from her brain and orient herself in the tight, warm nest where she woke.

Her first coherent thought was to recognize she wasn't alone in the snug space. A large, hard body pressed her into the soft folds of bedding.

Alec. Heart thundering, she twisted her body, shifting clumsily until she could see his face.

A lazy grin greeted her, and ocean-blue eyes peered out from half-lowered lids.

"Mornin', sweetcakes," Alec said, his craggy voice music to her ears.

"Alec! Are you all right?" She wiggled her hands up to feel for warmth in his stubbled cheeks.

"I'm fine. Damn fine at the moment, in fact." The healthy, pink glow in his skin and the fire that leaped in his gaze vouched for his recovery. Still, she skimmed her hands down his shoulders, over his chest and hips reassuring herself that his skin felt warm everywhere, that he had actually pulled through in good form. Every inch of him she touched radiated heat, filled their shared sleeping bag with cozy warmth.

She exhaled the air she'd been holding in her lungs and rolled closer to him, wrapping her arms around his neck. "Thank heavens. I was so scared. If anything had happened to you, I—"

The scrape of his calloused palm against her bare back stopped her short. He stroked his wide palm down her spine, cupped her fanny and nudged her closer. Closer to his naked chest, closer to his taut muscles, closer to the hard ridge at his groin.

Her breath snagged in her throat, and she lifted a wary, self-conscious gaze.

His smile brightened and mischief flashed in his eyes. "What's wrong, Erin? Never wake up in the same sleeping bag with a naked man before?"

"You're not naked," she choked out inanely.

"Near enough. And so are you." As if to prove his point, Alec skimmed his hand slowly back up her spine, his touch sparking her sensitive nerve endings like a live wire. At her nape, he plowed his fingers through her hair to capture her head. "Can't say that I know a more pleasant way to wake in the morning than next to the soft curves of warm woman."

Erin's heart kicked her ribs, and a hot pulse shot through her body.

Alec dipped his head and found her lips. He brushed a gentle kiss across her mouth, and a groan rumbled from his throat. "I could eat you up."

She chuckled. "Clearly you survived your dunk in an icy stream with no lasting ill effects."

"Mmm-hmm. Thanks to you."

A fresh slice of guilt doused the fluttery desire puddling in her belly. "I know. I'm sorry. I lost my balance and just grabbed for the first thing I could—"

He placed a finger on her lips to silence her. "I meant I owe you for getting me warm and keeping me alive after I went in the water."

Dubious of his praise, she studied his forgiving expression. "But it was my fault that you—"

"It was an accident. Stop blaming yourself." He rubbed her bottom lip with his finger, and the tender caress made her head spin and her limbs weak. "What matters is when I needed your help, you were grace under pressure and did everything exactly right. I know you were scared, but you kept your head and took care of me. You were magnificent."

Speechless, she stared into his eyes, and the tears she'd held at bay last night prickled her sinuses.

"You know what I think?" he asked, his voice a silky caress.

She shook her head, her throat too tight with emotion to talk.

"I think you're going to make a terrific mother."

His compliment stunned her, shook her. Rocked her to the roots of everything she'd believed about herself in the days since she learned of Joey Finley's death.

Her tears surged to her eyes in a wave. "Really?" she squeaked.

He kissed her leaky eyes and pulled her closer. "Yes, really. I don't waste my breath saying things I don't mean."

Alec's faith in her soothed her raw soul but stirred a different sort of ache deep in her bones—a longing for someone like him to share her life with, raise her child with, grow old with. She swallowed past the lump in her throat and tugged up the corner of her mouth. "That means a lot to me."

"I thought you needed to know. Things happen sometimes that are out of our control. Tragic things. But you proved yesterday that you've got what it takes to rise to the occasion when needed. That's what real courage is. And you've got it in spades, lady." The low, growling conviction of his tone burrowed to her heart as much as his words.

She opened her mouth to respond, but no sound came. Had anyone ever shown such faith in her, been so kind or encouraging? Not since her parents had died.

Before she could collect her thoughts, Alec closed the distance between them and caught her mouth with a soft kiss. The touch of his lips sent fresh sparks of desire shimmying through her. She slid her arms around his neck and responded with zeal, eager to show him with her kiss what she couldn't find the words to say. She suckled and drew on his bottom lip, teased his tongue with hers, and hummed her satisfaction when he deepened the kiss.

When he paused long enough for them to gasp for air, Alec locked a penetrating gaze on her. "Only two things are keeping me from making love to you right now," he rasped.

"What things?" She shook with the need and hunger for Alec's kiss. She wanted his hands on her skin and his body joined with hers.

"I need to know I won't hurt your baby." The sincerity and selflessness of his concern tripped through her and made her insides melt.

She pressed her forehead to his and smiled. "No. You won't hurt the baby."

"You're sure."

"I'm sure. What's the other thing?"

"I need to know I won't hurt you."

"Me? How could it hurt me?"

His set his jaw in the hard, grim manner that made the muscle in his cheek jump. "You don't strike me as the kind of woman who can give her body away without giving her heart."

"Oh."

"I don't do relationships, Erin," he said as his fingers trailed along the curve of her throat, over her shoulder, and down her back.

Delicious trills of anticipation followed in the wake of his touch. Her body quaked and hummed.

"I can't afford to become involved with a woman. Emotions and personal commitments are dangerous for me." His hand strummed back up her spine, and she could barely think, much less make sense of what he was saying.

"But if you understand this," he murmured, his tone thick

and seductive, "if you are willing to settle for mutually satisfying sex—" he unhooked her bra and brushed a whispery kiss on the tip of her nose "—between two consenting adults, then I can show you a good time."

She shivered with pleasure and expectation. "I have—" she jolted when his fingers slipped under the cup of her bra "—no doubt you can."

He nipped her chin, traced the line of her jaw with his tongue. "Is that a yes?"

When his hand closed around her bared breast and his thumb teased the tightened peak, her head grew muzzy, and she couldn't think. He tweaked her nipple, and lightning shot through her blood. She curled her fingers into the taut muscles of his shoulders and fought for a breath. "Don't stop."

"Roger that," he whispered and sealed their lips again, making her senses reel.

With a nudge, Alec pushed aside her bra, freeing her pregnancy-swollen breasts for his exploration. His nimble fingers cupped and caressed, tested and teased. His touch made her breasts tingle and tighten, sending spirals of liquid heat to her core.

He moved his kiss to the hollow below her ear, along her throat and down…down. When he reached her chest, nuzzling the valley between her breasts, Alec paused. She peeked up at him, puzzled why he'd stopped. In the watery morning light, he stared at her nakedness. The untamed hunger in his eyes stole her breath. Set her on fire.

Erin's breath shuddered from her on a shaky sigh. She ran her fingers through his mussed hair and savored the exquisite sensations he stirred with his hands, his mouth. Hooking her leg behind his knees, she raised her hips to grind against his, longing for more contact with his body. In response, he wedged a leg between hers, pressing his thigh high against the juncture of her legs. While he continued nibbling and kissing her breasts, her neck, her ears, Erin insinuated a hand between them and found the thick, rigid proof of his arousal. She closed her hand around him, and Alec bucked as if hit by an electric bolt. He sucked in a sharp breath and met her eyes with a gaze that was pure blue fire. With a grin tugging her lips, she drew one finger up the length of him, then back down. A growl of satisfaction rumbled from his chest, and she felt the shock wave that shuddered through him. His response to her was encouraging, empowering.

"Ah, sweetcakes, you're killin' me."

She smiled smugly. "Good."

Bracing on one trembling arm above her, Alec used his free hand to drag her panties down and invade her most intimate region. She arched into his hand, eager for his touch. He sank one finger deeper into her warmth and stroked until she thought she might fly apart. She clung to him, her body tense and vibrating, careening toward oblivion.

Then he stopped.

Pulling his hand away from her, he raised his head and grew still.

Erin almost wept with frustration. "Please, Alec…don't tease—"

He laid his fingers over her mouth and shushed her. "Do you hear that?"

All Erin heard was the pounding of the blood in her ears, the rasp of her shallow, agitated breathing. "No, I don't hear any—"

The low rumbling reached her, and she perked her ears to the sound.

"What time is it?" Alec asked as he grabbed her arm and turned her wrist to check her watch. He bit out a curse and flew into action.

"Get a move on, sweetcakes. That's our ride. We've got to

make tracks down to the pickup spot, or Jake'll leave without us."

Erin blinked at him in disbelief. "N-now? But we—"

"Now. Grab only what you *have* to take. No time to break camp." With quick, efficient moves, Alec found the sleeping-bag zipper and peeled open their snug cocoon.

The cold morning air hit her overheated and thrumming body like a slap. She gasped and bolted upright. Disappointment and unspent passion swirled through her, and she wanted to scream her frustration as she started gathering her clothes to dress. With effort, she squelched the urge to complain. They were both alive and rescue was imminent. So what if she'd lost the chance for a few moments of unbridled bliss with Alec?

Erin sighed, unconvinced. She still felt robbed of something precious and rare.

Alec grunted as he yanked a shirt over his head and paused long enough to roll his shoulders and rub his neck.

Pausing, she sent him a concerned glance. "Alec?"

"Just stiff muscles. Nothing a little heat and hydration won't fix." He slipped a finger under the strap of her bra and slid it up to her shoulder. Catching her chin between his fingers, he smacked a kiss on her mouth and gave her one of his intense, soul-shattering stares. "Later."

The accompanying heat in his eyes left no question what he intended for *later,* and the quivers of passion that had receded in her blood flashed hot again.

Once dressed, Alec snatched open the tent flaps and rushed outside. Erin scrambled to follow. She donned as many of the dry shirts as she could find and held the parka out for him. "Your turn to wear this."

He waved it away. "We'll be moving fast, making our own heat. The bulk will just slow me down. Grab that pack, and let's go."

As soon as she picked up the dry backpack, Alec took it from her, slung it over his shoulder and seized her hand. "Tell me if I go too fast for you."

With that, he turned and ran, hauling her along behind him.

Erin stumbled as she tried to keep up with his fast clip. No doubt, without her in tow, he'd be flying down the steep slope toward the helicopter.

The *whop-whop-whop* of the helicopter grew louder as they dashed down the mountain. Adrenaline alone kept Erin moving.

Within minutes they reached a clearing where a sleek helicopter sat, turbine rumbling and propellers spinning. Her pulse and her pace picked up speed as they darted out of the trees and made tracks across the snowy field to meet their ride.

They'd nearly reached the chopper when Alec stumbled to a stop. Reached for his gun. Shoved Erin down in the snow.

"Stay here. If anything happens, run for the trees and keep going."

Her heart slammed against her ribs and, winded from their run, she gasped for breath. "What's…wrong?"

Leading with his weapon, Alec approached the chopper. "That's not Jake!"

Chapter 10

As Alec charged the helicopter, the pilot whipped out his own gun, a large military-looking weapon that sent icy chills through Erin that had nothing to do with the snow she lay in. Her breath clouded in white puffs that obscured her view as she watched the tense standoff.

"Who are you? Where's Jake?" Alec shouted over the roar of the helicopter.

"Flu. He sent me." Machine gun still poised in one hand, the pilot flashed a badge of some sort. "Name's Carlisle. Oscar."

Alec motioned with his fingers. "Toss it here."

The pilot threw the badge toward Alec. Alec caught it and cautiously studied the I.D. while keeping an eye—and his gun—on the pilot.

Erin waited, her nerves doing a tap dance, her hands and feet growing numb from the cold.

Alec snapped the I.D. wallet closed, stared at Carlisle for a moment, then tossed the I.D. back. "Jake didn't sound sick when I talked to him."

The pilot shrugged. "I'm not a doctor. All I know is, he called me this morning and asked me to make the pickup. Said he had a fever of one-oh-three and a vicious cough."

Still Alec didn't seem satisfied.

Erin knew he operated in a world where trust wasn't a given, where betrayal was a deadly and constant threat. But his reluctance to go with the different pilot seemed overkill to Erin. Surely his secure connections and top-secret contacts were enough security.

Alec flicked a worried glance toward her, and she felt a kick in her chest. In that instant she knew—his overzealous caution was for *her*. Perhaps he thought he could risk trusting this unknown pilot if he was alone. He could probably even fly the helicopter for himself if needed. But her presence changed the situation. She was an inconvenient responsibility he had to factor into his assessment. A leadlike weight settled in her chest. The last thing she wanted was to be a liability to Alec. A problem.

"Who authorized the use of the chopper to come out here?" Alec called to the pilot.

The pilot chortled. "Who authorized it? Hell, this chopper's not even here. It's in the maintenance hangar back at Boulder at this very moment."

Alec's posture relaxed a degree, and he nodded in response to Carlisle's odd answer. Finally he trotted over to her and helped her to her feet. "Okay, we're going."

Erin frowned. "Did he mean he *stole* the helicopter?"

"*Stole* is such an unforgiving word," Alec said and tipped a grin at her. "*Borrowed* has a nicer ring."

"All in a day's work for a secret agent?" she asked, dusting snow from her clothes.

He cocked his head and lifted one eyebrow but said nothing. With her hand in his, he tugged her toward the waiting chopper. Alec settled in the seat beside her, then leaned toward the front long enough to confer with Carlisle.

The pilot nodded, flipped some switches, and soon the aircraft lifted smoothly into the sky. Erin held her stomach as they swooped around and swung in a wide arc, heading back toward civilization.

Alec took her hand and rubbed her fingers between his palms, much the way she had done for him the night before. The warm abrasion of his calloused palms on her cold hands soon had tingling heat flowing through her fingers again. Her thoughts jumped to the moments right before they'd heard the helicopter. Those same rough palms had scraped lightly over her breasts, her belly, her legs.

If their ride hadn't come, she had no doubt she'd have made love to Alec without a second thought. Until later.

The interruption of the arriving chopper had probably saved her from making a costly mistake. Alec was right. She couldn't make love without involving her heart. Joining her body with Alec's, no matter how blissful and sweet at the time, would have hurt her far more in the long run. They had no future together.

As she'd just witnessed, she was a liability to Alec.

When Alec found Daniel, found the men who'd set him up in South America, found the people trying to kill them, where would that leave her? When she no longer needed his protection, would he walk out of her life without a backward glance? Alec just wasn't the home, hearth and family type.

What's more, his dangerous, sometimes seamy lifestyle was not compatible with raising a child. She knew, better than most, the devastating cost of having a child idolize the wrong role model. She wanted her child to have a father figure, but that man couldn't be someone who jumped from moving vehicles on the interstate, or crashed airplanes to elude killers, or hunted terrorists in jungles. Alec simply wasn't the right man for her—or her baby.

Erin turned to watch the landscape below them and sighed. The truth was she needed to get out of Alec's life, out of his way, as soon as possible. When they landed, she'd tell him goodbye. If he felt she still needed to hide, she could go to a hotel, leave town, buy a disguise. But she wouldn't be a burden to him.

Her decision made, her throat clogged with emotion and sharp-edged regret sliced through her. She'd miss Alec. Despite his perilous lifestyle, he had a caring and gentle side that touched her. He was a man of courage, conviction. A man she could easily have fallen in love with under different circumstances.

Perhaps she'd even lost a bit of her heart to him already.

When Erin fell asleep against him, Alec battled down the barrage of seductive memories that assaulted him. Waking with her in his arms, feeling her warm skin against his, kissing his way down from her sweet mouth to her smooth shoulders and full breasts…

Making love to her, even though he'd warned her of his inability to give her more than the here and now, would have been colossally foolish. He already had a difficult time keeping his mind on his business when he was near Erin. And now he had her taste lingering on his tongue, the feel of her supple body burning his skin, the sound of her sighs echoing in his mind.

His blood still ran hot, and the simple brush of her silky hair on his cheek as she napped against his shoulder taunted him with what had *almost* happened between them. Being inside Erin would have been nirvana, he had no doubt. But dangers lurked even in paradise, and he had a responsibility to protect her, not jeopardize them both for the sake of sex, no matter how earthshaking it would have been.

He eased her head from his shoulder, resettling her with a folded-shirt pillow against the headrest, then slid up front into the copilot's seat. He put on a headset with a lip mic so he could talk to Carlisle.

The last-minute change in pilots had him on edge. The fewer people that knew he was alive, the better. And the fewer people who saw Erin with him, the better off she'd be, as well.

"What's our ETA into Boulder?"

"About ten more minutes." Carlisle tossed him a side glance. "Mind if I ask what you and your woman were doing up on that mountain in weather like this?"

"Yeah, I do."

The pilot snorted. "Fine. Never mind that I risked my ass to save yours."

Alec frowned at Carlisle. What did the guy want? A damn pat on the back? An *attaboy?*

The men and women who worked for the black ops team knew risk, secrecy and spur-of-the-moment assignments were part of the job. Carlisle's question rang warning bells that already vibrated warily.

Alec said little to Carlisle until the outskirts of Boulder came into view. As they made their approach to the private airstrip, Carlisle lifted the handset mic, changed the radio frequency and held it to his lips. "Charlie one-niner, this is Carlisle. ETA two minutes."

"Roger that, Carlisle. Good work," a new male voice, not the controller in the tower that had been on the radio moments earlier, replied.

Bristling, Alec nailed a narrow-eyed glare on the man at the controls. "Who the hell were you just talking to?"

"Just reporting in," the pilot said with a shifty grin.

If he'd had any doubt before that Carlisle wasn't who he

claimed, that someone had gotten to Jake and that his and Erin's cover had been blown, he didn't now. Carlisle's arrival announcement reeked of a setup. Icy prickles scraped down Alec's spine.

He seized the smirking man by the throat and growled, "Who was on the radio?"

The chopper lurched, and Carlisle's face twisted in an ugly snarl. "Let go of me, or I swear I'll crash this chopper and kill us all."

Alec had called men's bluff in more precarious situations than this. But never with the life of a pregnant woman he'd sworn to protect on the line.

Carlisle groped next to his seat and swung a Ruger P-series pistol up, jamming it under Alec's chin. "Let go, you bastard," he rasped.

Alec relaxed his grip on the man's neck, but every other muscle in his body knotted, and his nerves jumped. When they landed, he was certain they would be attacked.

He sank back into the copilot seat and weighed his options, knowing he was losing valuable time to make his next move. His choice would have been obvious had Erin not been on board. He knew how to fly a helicopter, and Carlisle was expendable. But before he enacted any plan, he needed to review it for anything that would put Erin at unreasonable risk. His own life, he'd gamble. Erin's was a different matter.

His hesitation sawed through him, went against all his training. Indecision or hesitation in the field could prove a costly mistake. A quick glance out the window to the landing strip settled the matter for him. A small posse of armed men waited to meet them. *Hell.*

From his peripheral vision, he monitored Carlisle. The instant the pilot shifted his gaze to the controls in preparation to land, Alec struck. A swift upward arc of his elbow knocked Carlisle's gun hand up. The pilot tensed, firing the gun into the roof.

Erin woke with a scream.

Alec followed quickly with a knockout punch across Carlisle's jaw.

The pilot wilted in his seat, and as the helicopter controls slid from the unconscious man's grip, the helicopter dipped sharply.

"Alec!"

"Change of plans. Hold on and stay low!" he shouted to her as he grabbed the copilot controls. Pulling the cyclic, he swung the chopper around, sending them up and away from the landing strip—and the goon arrival party. Bullets pocked the windshield and dinged the nose of the chopper.

Erin gasped and shrunk to the floor of the back seat.

Sweat beaded on Alec's lip. One bullet in the gas tank, and it'd be all over for him. For Erin and her unborn child. Protectiveness surged through him with a wrath that shook him. Grinding his teeth until his jaw ached, he focused his energy on flying the helicopter.

"What happened? Who were they?" Erin called over the rumble of the turbine.

"I don't know," he grated. "Hang on. I'm going to dump some ballast."

Alec swung the chopper low over an empty field and shoved Carlisle, unconscious and limp, out of the aircraft.

"He wasn't one of your men after all?" Erin stared, wide-eyed at the man sprawled on the frozen ground below.

"No." Maneuvering the cyclic stick again, Alec set a course headed north, mentally estimating the best city to ditch the chopper and hop a flight to Houston or New Orleans. They'd have to be careful, find some new clothes to disguise themselves.

If the greeting they'd received in Boulder proved nothing

else, it made clear one truth. He'd have to keep Erin with him a little longer. Until he knew who was behind the attempts on his life and he'd eliminated that threat, he wouldn't leave Erin unprotected. She was in the situation because of him, and he wouldn't rest until he was certain she was safe.

"Ever been to Louisiana, sweetcakes?"

Clearing her throat, she said, "I had a layover in New Orleans once. Otherwise, no."

In light of the events of the past twenty-four hours, she'd done admirably keeping her composure. The woman was made of tougher stuff than she gave herself credit for. She was a dangerously intriguing blend of courage and compassion, mettle and marshmallow, sugar and spice.

Alec's body thrummed along with the helicopter engine, remembering his taste of Erin's *spice* that morning. Groaning, he turned his attention out the windshield. With Erin along as he hunted down the location Daniel marked on the Louisiana map, he might get the chance to finish what they'd started that morning. If he dared.

He already liked Erin far too much, cared too deeply about what happened to her. And Erin deserved more than a sexual fling with a man who could only give her here and now.

"How did they find us, Alec?" Erin's tremulous question sobered him, cutting through the haze of lust that had engulfed him. When he glanced over his shoulder, the fright he saw in her eyes slapped him with the truth. His first priority was keeping Erin safe, not ravishing her.

"My guess is the person who sold Daniel and me out in Colombia is closer to the team than I'd originally thought. Maybe even within our ranks. We'll have to consider everyone as suspect until I can root out the bastard." Alec's stomach turned at the notion of a traitor on the team, and bile burned his throat.

While he stewed over the betrayal, Alec flew the chopper to an isolated landing zone near Cheyenne. Before heading to the airport, they bought new clothes at a consignment shop. Alec added wire-rimmed glasses and a baseball cap to his disguise and handed Erin a blond wig and scarf when she came out of the ladies' dressing room wearing her new gauzy skirt and blouse. She looked ready to object, but she obviously recalled the men who'd opened fire on them in Boulder and took the wig silently.

When their flight landed in New Orleans, Alec rented a car for them using a fake name and driver's license, and they headed west, following the directions Daniel had laid out on the back of the pirate's map.

As they drove through the marshlands of southern Louisiana, Alec recalled the stories Daniel had told him about growing up on the bayou, raised by his *grandmere*. A strange twinge plucked his chest, a sense of longing he experienced whenever Daniel talked of his home and his family. A similar feeling had prodded him as he watched Erin stroke her belly and listened to her talk of her baby, her parents, her life in Cherry Creek. In the past few days, the longing had grown to a dull ache lodged squarely in his chest.

"Beautiful," Erin said, rousing Alec from his thoughts. Her attention was riveted on the sight outside the car window— moss-draped cypress trees and boggy waterways where egrets waded, waiting for a fish to swim by. "Beautiful and yet kind of spooky. Mysterious."

"Mmm-hmm. I have to warn you. If this place Daniel is directing us to is half as isolated and decrepit as the places he's told me about in the past, you may be in for a shock. The swamps have alligators and flying bugs and no electricity. The Cajuns that moved here centuries ago built shacks on stilts, deep in the bayous and accessible only by pirogue."

Alec pulled off the road at a small wooden building with

a handmade sign that read Gambeaux's—Bait for Sale. Hot and Spicy Crawfish by the Pound.

"Pirogue?" Erin asked.

"A kind of flat boat guided through the water using a long pole. You'll see soon enough. That's how we'll be traveling from here."

Erin squinted out the window at the tiny, run-down shack. On the wooden dock behind the building, an older man tossed something into the water, and an alligator lunged through the water to snap up the offered meat.

Erin shivered. "This is it?"

Alec double-checked his GPS locator. The coordinates matched the instructions Daniel had detailed on his map. "It's our next-to-last stop." He pointed to the dense, shadowed swamp and maze of knobby cypress trees. "Our final destination is out there somewhere."

Chapter 11

As they entered the old bait shop, the sulfur and dead-fish smells of the swamp made Erin's stomach roil. She pressed a hand to her mouth while Alec spoke to the elderly man they'd seen on the dock about renting a pirogue.

"Mais oui!" the old man said, shuffling outside with a homemade wooden cane and waving his hand toward several rickety boats. "Pawpaw has *beaucoup* pirogues for you. Choose."

The man's accent and sprinkled use of Cajun French intrigued Erin. Alec stepped over to examine the floating vessels and hitched his thumb toward one of the better ones. "How much for this one? We'll need it for several days."

A fat black-and-white cat strolled out from the bait shop and rubbed against Erin's leg. "Hello, kitty," Erin said, squatting to scratch the cat's chin while Alec negotiated with the old man.

"Comment tu crois? Gumbo done found hisself *un ami, oui?"* the man said with a chuckle.

"Yes." Erin gave the cat a final pat the dusted the hair from her hands as she stood. "He's a friendly fella."

"Gumbo *est beaucoup amoureux, cher!* A womanizer!"

Erin grinned at the old man, and Alec slipped him a few bills before helping her climb into the chosen pirogue. She lowered herself uneasily onto the dusty, splintered wooden seat and cast an uneasy glance into the murky water. Lord only knew what types of slithery creatures lurked in the muddy swamp.

When Alec climbed into the boat, the pirogue rocked, and Erin clutched the sides.

"The missus don' look like she so sure 'bout dis." The old man flashed a gap-toothed grin.

Erin's already queasy stomach took an extra flip hearing the man refer to her as Alec's wife. She sent the man a tired smile, the best she could manage with her nerves strung as tight as banjo strings.

"Don' worry, *cher,*" the old man said, tapping the edge of the flatboat with his cane, "Pawpaw give you good pirogue. His best."

Alec unlooped the rope tied to the dock and tossed it on the floor at his feet.

"Thank you, sir," he said with a nod, then pushed them out into the swamp with the long narrow oar the man had given him for steering the pirogue through the water.

A mosquito buzzed by Erin's ear, and she swatted at it. The sun was setting rapidly, and the bony arms of cypress trees and veil of Spanish moss cast long shadows on the algae-covered bayou.

Lulled by the gentle lapping of the bayou against the hull, Erin tried to unwind a bit. But as they skimmed through the knobby roots and tall marsh grasses, she felt almost as if the bayou were alive and watching their every move. *Paranoia,* she told herself, remnants of their escape from the armed men earlier in the day and their attempts to disguise themselves.

Alec handed her the small GPS device. "Read me the co-ordinates as we go. It can't be too far from here."

Erin appreciated having something semi-useful to do as they made their way through the shadowy bayou. Strange buzzes, croaks and groans sounded all around her, and every creaking tree and distant splash set her more on edge.

"There." Alec pointed to something behind her. "I think that's it."

Pivoting on the small wooden seat, Erin peered through the dim bayou to the ramshackle hut on stilts that loomed over the water ahead of them. "You're kidding, right? That's not really where we're spending the night."

"Don' worry, *cher.* Gators no climb ladders." Alec mimicked the old Cajun who'd rented them the pirogue. The quick flash of white teeth as Alec grinned did little to settle her nerves.

"Yeah, but what about snakes? And spiders? They can drop out of trees and…" Erin shivered.

The boat rocked slightly, and she felt a warm hand on her shoulder. "I won't let any creepy crawlies get you, Erin. I promise."

She gave herself a mental shake, ashamed of herself for burdening Alec with her petty phobias. He'd risked life and limb to keep her safe thus far, and she had no doubt he would continue. Even if doing so made his own life more difficult. His sacrifices on her behalf were humbling.

Alec steered the pirogue up to the tiny floating dock at the foot of the stilts. The rotting wood slats of the dock creaked when he helped her step out of the boat. Alec finished tying off the pirogue and joined her on the dock. Putting a hand at her waist, he steadied her, and his reassuring presence soothed the jitters scrambling in her gut.

They climbed a ladder made of small chunks of plywood nailed to one of the stilts, and as she hoisted herself onto the elevated floor of the shack, Erin peered warily inside. Despite the hovel's ratty outward appearance, the interior did boast a few creature comforts. A bed. A desk cluttered with papers. A small sink. Shelves lined with canned food and supplies. "Looks like Daniel's been here. The place is supplied and furnished."

"Either that or he was expecting us." Alec lit a kerosene lantern and hung it on a nail by the door.

A warm, yellow light filled the room and made the space feel oddly homey and comforting to Erin. Or maybe it was simply Alec's solid strength and commanding presence that caused the quiet calm that stole through her. For the first time in hours, her muscles relaxed, and she drew a steadying breath.

Until she turned to find Alec staring at the bed in the corner of the room. Fire leaped in his eyes. *Later.*

The heat that radiated from Alec mirrored the passion with which he'd made his one-word promise that morning. Her gaze flicked nervously to the one bed, as well. Images and sensations from that morning assaulted her, left her trembling. That morning she'd acted impulsively, swept away by the sensual press of Alec's body against hers, still shell-shocked from Alec's brush with hypothermia and longing for the life-affirming experience of making love to Alec.

Now, with time and distance, she had no such excuses for the internal pull that drew her to this man. For the tender ache that burgeoned in her chest. For the need to share herself with this man. No excuse other than the truth. She had deep feelings for Alec that went beyond friendship or gratitude or lust. Dear heavens, was she falling in love with him?

"You said earlier that you were hungry," Alec said, although the husky timbre of his voice let her know that food wasn't what was foremost on his mind.

She nodded and rubbed a hand over her belly. "Starved."

"Let's find you and Junior something before you pass out on me then." He moved over to the shelves and pulled down a can. "Beets." He grunted and put that can back to try for another. "Spaghetti and meatballs. Now we're talking." He glanced over his shoulder. "Sound okay?"

A sensation like warm honey puddled behind her ribs then spread through her limbs, seeped to her core. The way Alec took care of her, put her needs before his own, rooted deep in her soul. Her life with Bradley would have been so different if he'd given her needs and wishes the same consideration.

"Spaghetti is fine." She crossed the room and put a hand on his forearm. Meeting his eyes, she squeezed his arm and smiled. "Thank you."

His brief hesitation, the little nod and tug at the corner of his mouth, told her he knew she was thanking him for more than dinner. She kept a firm grip on his arm, bracing herself when a barrage of sensation swamped her. Admiration. Wonder. And a unique sense of contentment and fulfillment she wasn't sure she'd ever known before.

Alec challenged her, pampered her, made her every fiber feel completely feminine and fully alive.

"It's been a rather harrowing day for you. Why don't you rest while I get this heated up?" Alec tipped his head toward the small camping stove on the counter by the sink.

She grinned. "Harrowing? Yeah." Her lips twitched in amusement. "Is life with you ever anything but harrowing?"

A harder, darker emotion wiped the humor from his face.

"Danger is a fact of life for me. Because of my job, my training." His expression closed, grew cool and distant as he turned away to open the canned spaghetti.

This reminder splashed a cold dose of reality on her wayward thoughts.

He sighed heavily. "I'm sorry I brought you into the line of fire."

"You didn't. Manny and whoever hired him did. You've done nothing but look out for me from the day we met."

In the past several days, she'd seen so many sides of Alec. A man who could be ruthless and dangerous or gentle and kind. A man of cunning, intelligence and resourcefulness. But he was a man with secrets, too. A man with vulnerabilities that he guarded and shoved down in self-defense. Erin ached to chip through the stony, protective facade and touch the soul of the man whose hurt and private darkness she'd glimpsed in moments when she caught him off guard. She longed to give him the comfort and healing she knew he needed but would never seek on his own. But she knew, in his eyes, opening himself to her, showing his vulnerabilities would be a show of weakness, so she didn't push.

While Alec set to work lighting the camping stove and opening a few cans for their dinner, Erin strolled around the small cabin, peeking into closets and cabinets and giving the small bed a test bounce. The mattress proved remarkably firm and comfortable.

Turning her attention to the cluttered desk in the corner, she sifted through a collection of articles and papers spread across the top. She frowned, noticing most were clippings about the Louisiana senator whose daughter had been kidnapped. She found a notepad, too, with various notes scribbled and flowcharts with the senator's name, the senator's daughter and General Ramirez each in a circle with lines drawn in a triangle connecting each name to the others.

A tingle started down her spine. "Ramirez? But he's—" Erin pivoted toward Alec. "That rebel army general you and

Daniel were watching in Colombia on your last mission together? His name was Ramirez, right?"

"Yeah, why?" Alec turned from the camping stove, and his eyes zeroed in on the papers in her hands. "What did you find?"

Gaze narrowing, he crossed the floor to her, and Erin showed him the diagram. "It looks like Daniel was working on a theory that connects Senator White, his missing daughter and Ramirez."

Alec shoved the spoon he'd been stirring spaghetti with into Erin's hand and started riffling through the papers on the desk. "What were you on to, Lafitte?"

From the newspaper clippings and photocopied pages, Alec pulled out a high school yearbook.

"Lagniappe High School Fighting Mudbugs," Erin read aloud. "Is that where Daniel went to high school?"

"No." Alec flipped the yearbook open to the first page that had been bookmarked. Nicole White's senior picture had been circled.

Erin leaned closer to study the picture over Alec's shoulder. "The senator's daughter. She's pretty."

"Yeah." Alec studied the photo a moment longer before flipping to the next marked page. Nicole White was pictured with the cheerleaders on the right page and with the debate team on the left page. Five other spots featuring Nicole's varied activities were marked, as well.

"If you ask me, I think Daniel has a thing for Nicole White."

Alec jerked his eyebrows together. "Why do you say that?"

She waved a hand toward the collection of photos and articles spread on the desk. "Well, look at everything he's collected on her."

Alec shook his head and tossed the yearbook on the desk. "Research. When we were hunting Ramirez, we studied pictures of him so we could memorize his face, his distinguishing features. Standard operating procedure. He's got pictures here of Senator White and Ramirez, too."

"A couple. But he's got one, two, three, four…" Erin shuffled through the papers and continued counting silently. "Twelve pictures of Nicole. And tons more background information on her."

Alec scowled and plucked out a blown-up copy of a recent shot of Nicole. "I see your point."

Erin slid Daniel's diagram out of the clutter again. "Maybe I'm wrong. But do you think he suspected Nicole of having ties to Ramirez? That she could have been selling U.S. secrets or something she'd stolen from her father's office? I mean her mission trip could have been a cover. What if she wasn't really kidnapped but actually disappeared because she was working with Ramirez?"

"Anything's possible. In my line of work, you learn not to dismiss any scenario as too far-fetched. But—"

A loud sizzle from the stove drew her attention away from what Alec was saying.

"The spaghetti!" She rushed over to the stove and snatched the smoking pan off the burner.

Alec scowled and took the pan from her. "Sorry. Guess I set the burner too high. I'll fix something else."

She stopped him before he could dump the pan. "It's not totally ruined, and I'm too hungry to wait on anything else."

"Erin—"

She grinned. "Trust me, Alec. This baby is not picky when it comes to *what* I eat and completely impatient about *when*. This is fine." She looked on the shelf by the sink for a bowl. "Are you joining me?"

"Nah. I'll get something later."

Finding another spoon but no bowl, Erin carried the spaghetti to the corner of the bed and ate from the pan. Alec strolled to the pile of papers on the desk and studied them with a pensive knit in his brow.

"What?" she asked.

He brushed a few of the top sheets back and picked up the notepad on which Daniel had jotted notes. "I'll be damned."

"Alec?" Setting the pan of scorched spaghetti aside, Erin crossed to the desk to see what Alec had found.

"A lot of things are clearer to me now." He showed her the page of Daniel's scribblings that had caught his attention. This diagram was set up differently but had the same three names linked. With two additions. Blackbeard and Lafitte. A line had been drawn from his and Daniel's nicknames to Senator White's name. On the opposite side of the page, a line connected Nicole's name to Ramirez. The two entries were connected in the middle of the sheet with a New Orleans street address and date.

Erin pointed to the date. "January sixth. That's next week. What do you think it means?"

"I can't be sure. But you can bet I'm going to be at this address on January sixth to find out."

An hour later, Erin had finished eating, had napped for a few minutes, taken a cold shower in the shack's primitive, no-hot-water bathroom and felt somewhat human again. But Alec still pored over the information Daniel had amassed, studying charts and lists and making notes of his own.

Erin approached the desk and gave Alec's hunched shoulders a deep rub. He moaned and rolled his neck from side to side as she massaged his kinked muscles. "You're playing with fire, sweetcakes."

"Pardon?"

He caressed her cheek with the back of his hand, his eyes homing in with bright blue intensity. "I want you, Erin. So bad it hurts. Ever since we broke camp this morning, I've thought of little else except you and how good you felt in my arms, how sweet you tasted." He tugged her closer, and she canted against him, feeling his body vibrate with leashed passion and power. When he nuzzled her neck and nipped at her earlobe, shivery sparks shot through her bloodstream.

"Now we can finish what we started this morning." He pressed delicate kisses along her jaw and strummed her spine with seductive strokes. "But I won't do anything unless you tell me it's still what you want, too."

Through the sensual haze he conjured with his kisses, a bittersweet pang pierced her bubble of contentment. She rested her forehead against his chest, inhaling the musky scent of aftershave she'd forever associate with Alec. "I want to make love to you as much as I want my next breath. But…"

His hold on her waist tightened. "But…?"

She lifted her chin to meet his gaze again, a hollow ache swelling inside her. "But I also know that I care about you too much to make love and have it mean nothing except great sex. I know I promised you this morning I could keep my emotions separate, but I don't think I can anymore. I need more from you than just sex, Alec."

Tensing, Alec dropped his hands from her and shook his head. "Erin, our lives are completely incompatible. I can't make promises about tomorrow or next week, much less further down the line. I told you—"

She silenced him with a finger over his lips. "I don't expect you to change your life for me. You've already done so much to protect me, and I won't ask for more." The tender ache twisted, driving deeper. "But I can't give you what you want, either, Alec. I can't sleep with you and keep my heart uninvolved. You already mean too much to me, and I don't know how I'm going to tell you goodbye when the time comes."

Alec's eyes slid closed, and he pressed his lips in a thin, taut line.

She cupped her hand against his cheek, and he covered her hand, lacing their fingers.

"I'm sorry, Alec," she said, her voice breaking. "But I've already loved and lost one man whose purpose in life was to taunt death, to push the limits and chase the next adrenaline high. I can't do that again."

He squeezed her fingers. "I know. I understand."

Tears burned her eyes, and she blinked them back. "You asked what I wanted. I want you, Alec. So much. But what I want and what I need aren't the same things. I *need* a quiet, safe life where I can raise my baby." She paused and pulled in a deep breath, debating the wisdom of broaching the issue weighing on her heart. "Maybe the question should be…what do *you* need, Alec?"

He stiffened, then stepped back. "Me?"

"You *are* half of this equation. This morning, you said you don't do relationships because of the dangers of your job. Is your life, with all the risks you face, really what you want?"

Alec's jaw tightened, and pain flashed in his eyes. "My life is what it is, Erin. What I want is irrelevant."

"Why? Don't you deserve to be happy?"

Alec spun away, plowing his hands through his hair with a huff. "We don't always get what we deserve from life. Much less what we want. Sometimes fate hands us crap, and we have to make do."

Erin heard a load of heartache in his voice and absorbed it deep into her marrow. "Who hurt you, Alec? What did fate do to steal your hope?"

He stalked past her and snatched his gun and holster from a small table. Without another word, he shouldered his way through the front door, disappearing outside.

In the silence of the dim bayou hideout, Erin sank onto the floor and wept for the man who held so much pain inside.

Chapter 12

A strange noise from the bayou woke Erin in the predawn hours. Shaking off her slumber, she stared into the blackness surrounding her and listened. When the eerie screeching reverberated in the dark again, Erin bolted upright in the bed, heart thumping.

"It was a bird. Probably an owl." Alec's quiet baritone voice drifted through the night like a balmy marshland breeze. "Don't be scared."

"I'm not. I…" She hesitated and drew a ragged breath.

"Your pulse is racing." He squeezed her wrist gently to let her know denial was futile, that the scattered throb under his fingers was proof of her heart rate.

Okay, maybe the shadowed bayou she'd seen last night, and the odd noises filling the pitch of night *did* creep her out. But she wasn't scared. Or at least she had no need to be. Alec was here. The heat and weight of his hand on her arm calmed and reassured her.

He drew her into the circle of his arms and rested his chin on her shoulder, her cheek to his. "Better?"

She felt her muscles relax, and she melted into his protective warmth. "Mmm-hmm. Thanks."

The steady thump of Alec's heart drummed against her back, and his thumb stroked the inside of her wrist, stirring a sweet lethargy in her bones.

"Why do you always smell like vanilla ice cream?" he murmured.

"Do I?"

"Mmm-hmm, you do." He angled his head to brush a kiss along her cheek.

Her skin tingled with a prickly, restless heat, while her lungs squeezed with regret. "Alec, I told you why I couldn't..." She sighed. "Nothing's changed."

She wiggled to get away from him, and his grip tightened, drawing her more firmly against his hard strength and heat. "Don't go. Please. I—"

"Alec, I can't. Not without falling in love with you."

She felt a small, almost imperceptible, shudder reverberate through his muscles, and her heart clenched.

"I...gave a lot of thought to what you said last night," he whispered.

She held her breath.

"And I can't say anything's changed. My job still makes it impossible for us to have a future together. But...I wanted you to understand some things about me...." He took a few quick, shallow breaths, and the drumming of his heartbeat against her back accelerated. "Things I've never told anyone else."

Erin stayed silent, giving him the time and patience he needed to say whatever had him so agitated.

"When I was fourteen, my mom used to pick me up at school after track practice. But um...one day, she...didn't come. I thought she was just late, but then it started to get dark and cold, so I walked home. When I got to our place, she—" Alec shifted restlessly behind her, his palms growing damp against her arms.

"Tell me, Alec. Please."

He sighed. "She was…gone."

Her chest tightened. "She was dead?"

He snorted derisively. "No. She'd packed up her things and moved out. She ditched me. I haven't seen her since."

Horror and anguish for the young Alec contracted Erin's chest. Her throat tightened, imagining his pain over his mother's betrayal and desertion.

"I stayed at our apartment, pretending everything was fine, dodging children's services, until the landlord kicked me out."

"And then?"

He drew a slow breath. "I lived on the streets. Learned real quick how to survive, how to defend myself, how to scrape past the cops."

Learned to put defensive walls around his heart. Learned not to trust people. Alec's teenage years explained a lot about his distant manner and the pain she saw in his eyes at unguarded moments. She lost another tiny piece of her soul to him, wishing she could heal his hurts. "What about your father? Where was he?"

Alec hesitated. "My mom never knew who my father was. He was one of many one-night stands."

Erin's stomach pitched, and grief knotted around her heart. She hated to think how scared and lonely Alec had been, abandoned by the woman who should have loved him most.

"I dropped out of school when I was sixteen," he recounted clinically. "I figured out I could make more money working odd jobs than sitting in a classroom all day."

Erin grimaced. "But school's important…."

He gave her a short, bittersweet laugh. "Said the dedicated teacher." He brushed his fingers along her cheek, adding,

"Maybe if I'd had a teacher like you, someone who really cared, I'd have done things differently. But I was on my own."

Her eyes watered as she tried to fathom the odds Alec had overcome, the hardships he'd endured at such a young age. She laced her fingers with his in support and nodded. "Go on."

"When I was eighteen, I joined the army. I figured I already knew how to fight and defend myself, so I might as well get paid for it. Have somewhere to live, something to eat. The army was my meal ticket, so I gave it everything I had. About the time the war in Iraq started, the officers offered me the chance to train to be a Ranger."

"That's where you learned all your action-hero tricks and skills, huh?" Her attempt to infuse a note of humor in her tone fell flat.

"I learned how to complete the most difficult missions and get out alive. Whatever it took." His voice darkened, grew more detached. "I learned how to kill. I won't glamorize my training."

Erin shivered. "What happened during the war?"

Alec drew a slow breath. The stillness of the predawn morning seemed to echo the edgy anticipation jangling inside her.

"When the most dangerous missions came up, I was always first to volunteer. Not because I had a death wish, mind you, but because I had no reason not to be the one to go. The other guys had parents, wives, kids. Someone to live for. I had nothing. No one." Alec's empty, emotionless tone wrenched inside Erin, deepening her sorrow for his lonely past.

"Oh, Alec…"

"I could go into a volatile situation without anything holding me back." He paused, sighed wearily. "After a few missions, I was pegged to join the black ops agency. The same circumstances that made me the best choice for Ranger missions made me perfect for high-risk counterterrorism work."

"The same circumstances." Tears climbed Erin's throat, choking her. "Meaning you were alone. Had no family."

Alec hesitated. "Yeah. I was expendable."

Erin sucked in a sharp breath and twisted toward him. "No! Alec, don't say that. You're *not* expendable. How could you think that!"

His eyes were as expressionless and dead as his voice. He turned from her to stare up at the ceiling. "My mother thought so."

Erin gave a hiccuping sob. "Damn her for hurting you! For abandoning you…"

The corner of his mouth twitched in a sarcastic grin. "I have. Lots of times. But after a while, I figured, what's the point? This is the life fate dealt me. And I realized I could use my isolation, my independence for some good. And I am good, Erin. I'm one of the best agents on the team."

"I believe that." She gave him a sad grin. "I've seen you in action, remember." She curled her fingers into the T-shirt that stretched across his broad chest. She trembled a bit, thinking of the dangerous life he'd led and the harsh training that had given him his impressive muscles and strength.

"I gave everything I had to the black ops team for seven years. Because I had nothing else." He expelled a harsh breath, and his brow furrowed. His lip curled, then tightened as he fought some dark emotion. "Or so I thought…until I left Daniel in Colombia. Then I realized that over the years we'd worked together, put our lives in each other's hands, I'd taken for granted the one thing I believed I'd never have."

He paused, and a quiver started in her gut. A niggling comprehension and fresh pain.

"I had someone's loyalty. His trust. I had a friend." Alec pressed the heels of his palms to his eyes. "But I left him. Just like my mom left me. I abandoned the only friend I had. I just left him to die…" His voice cracked as his emotions overtook him, and Erin's heart broke along with it. "To *hell* with our agreement not to compromise the mission," he grated. "Lafitte was my friend!"

His guilt and agony raked through her, shredding Erin's composure. She'd bet her child's life Alec was terrified of the emotions he was finally acknowledging. His willingness to share this turbulent part of himself, to open an emotional vein for her, was humbling. He'd reached into her soul and destroyed her capacity to fight her feelings for him.

"Oh, Alec…." She wrapped her arms around him and held him close, wishing she could take away his pain. "Don't punish yourself. Daniel's alive. He has to be. He sent you that letter. He's been here in the bayou recently. You even said so."

He released a shuddering sigh. "I know. I'm just so…tired, Erin," he rasped.

She raised her head to meet his gaze.

"So tired of—" He stopped. Swallowed hard. Shifting bleak, damp eyes to her, he shook his head. "Forget it."

"Of being alone?" she finished, understanding him. Maybe more than he was ready to acknowledge for himself.

Squeezing his eyes closed, he whispered, "You asked me what I needed."

Erin held her breath.

"I need you, Erin. I need…the connection I feel with you."

Hot moisture stung the back of her nose, and she bit her lip, fighting the rush of tears.

"I felt something the moment Manny cracked that branch on your head, and you looked at me with such sweet faith and innocence. I tried to shut it out, like I've always shut people out. But the hurt and betrayal in your eyes when you thought I'd put Daniel's letter over your life…it shattered something inside me. Made me see what I'd become. How isolated. How numb." He swiped the dampness from her cheek with his thumb. "The last few years of my life have been about death and lies and evil. But in you, I saw…maybe my last chance to save myself, to save my humanity. You were everything good and innocent and full of life. My God, you're even carrying a new life inside you. And I need that. I need…the way you make me feel. Alive. Connected to the things that matter."

Erin framed his face with her hands and rested her forehead against his. "I'm here, Alec. For whatever you need. Always. I promise."

He sank fingers into her hair, holding her close and covering her face with achingly tender kisses. Desperate kisses. Kisses full of affection and emotion and words left unsaid. Words that hovered near the surface. Words she saw reflected in his azure eyes.

She felt the tremor that shook him, and her body answered with a quaking need and clambering hunger. She held him tighter, angling her hips and shifting her legs, wishing she could climb inside him. Fill him. Give him all the love he'd been denied and had denied himself for too many years.

Alec's kisses drifted to her lips, and he groaned as he deepened the connection. Without breaking the seal of their kiss, Alec hooked a leg around hers and rolled her to her back. When his body pinned hers, he raised his head and stared deep into her eyes. Searching. Reaching to her soul. "Erin, if I don't make love to you, at least once, it's something I'll regret…forever."

Her breath caught. She knew he was asking permission. Giving her the chance to walk away. Like everyone else in his life had.

I need you, Erin. Her heart stumbled, braced. Prepared for retreat.

Could she do it? Could she give herself, heart and soul,

to this man? Because there'd be no going back for her if she made love to him. She knew that with painful certainty.

But when they found Daniel and the danger to her had passed, he would move on. Leave her behind. He'd told her nothing had changed in that respect. His high-risk lifestyle had no room for a wife and family.

Yet, despite what it would cost her heart, how could she not give him this gift? A few moments of knowing how it felt to be well and truly loved. The deep connection with a soul that wanted and cherished him.

The truth was, she already cared too deeply about him. When this was all over, when he left and went back to his job, she would feel the loss. To her core. She swallowed hard to force down the lump of heartache that swelled in her throat. "Make love to me, Alec."

Releasing an unsteady breath, he closed his eyes, bowed his head. As if collecting his composure. Or praying. When he raised his head, his expression was pure humility. Reverence. Awe.

Placing a soft kiss on her forehead, he slid his hands down her shoulders and arms and caught the hem of her gauzy shirt. Alec peeled her blouse over her head, stripping her of clothes as surely as he peeled away any defenses left to protect her heart. The skirt and her panties followed, leaving her naked to him, body and soul.

He caressed her with loving, desire-warm eyes and with tender fingers that roamed over every inch of her skin. Testing, learning, arousing. His slow, methodical strokes sent sparks of pleasure skittering over her skin and electrified every cell he touched.

Eager to feel his skin against hers, Erin tugged his T-shirt up, bunching it in her fingers. As he rose, straddling her hips, to toss the shirt aside, she grappled with trembling fingers to unbutton his jeans. The watery morning light seeped through the blinds, providing just enough illumination for her to study the planes and angles of his beautiful male body. The man personified strength and power. Agility and sensual grace. Her heart thumped harder as he moved back toward her like a panther stalking its prey.

But for all his savage beauty, the gentleness and passion in his eyes reverberated to her core. He moved aside long enough to strip off his jeans. Then, twining her limbs with his, she met his mouth and melted into his kiss. Sweet for a moment, then increasingly fervid, Alec tantalized her lips before moving down her body. The sexy rasp of his unshaven jaw played an enticing counterpoint to the satiny warmth of his lips and tongue as he skimmed over her breasts and nuzzled her belly. He nipped playfully at her hip, and as he made a pass over the tiny bulge where her baby grew, his kisses deepened, slowed.

Her throat closed with emotion watching him turn his head to brush his cheek against her belly, eyes closed and an expression of love and wonder softening his chiseled face. He placed one last soft kiss against her womb before sliding his hands up, along her sides, until he framed her face.

Alec's quick, shallow breaths mirrored hers, and he murmured her name on a slow exhale as he positioned himself for entry. Then, seizing her lips with a kiss she felt to her marrow, Alec joined their bodies. He filled her, stroking her with his heat and carrying her to dizzying heights. Farther. Faster. Higher.

All the while, his fathomless blue gaze clung to hers, binding their spirits along with their bodies.

Trembling and lost in the depth of love in his eyes, she tumbled over the precipice, free-falling, caught in a vortex of bliss and light. Tears blurred her vision as her world rocked, shifted, re-centered. Alec dropped his forehead to hers, and his hold on her tightened. He shuddered, a primal growl rumbling from his chest. Then he grew quiet. Still.

So still.

She stroked his head, held him close. Waited.

"Alec?" Not yet completely recovered herself, Erin's voice shook.

"Oh, God," he half whispered, half moaned.

Panic flared in her chest. "Alec? Are you all right?"

She shoved on his shoulders, needing to look into his eyes, gauge his expression.

"No." He dragged a hand through his hair and groaned again. "I'm not."

"What?"

When he raised his head from her shoulder, he looked haggard, shell-shocked. "I don't think I'll ever be all right again. I never thought… I didn't know—"

Erin's stomach pitched. "You have regrets. You think this was a mistake. You—"

"No." His tone and the drill of his gaze dispelled those doubts in an instant. "I regret nothing." He pulled in a deep breath and rested his forehead against hers again. Nose to nose, he sighed. "I simply miscalculated my ability to…handle this. How I'd react to being inside you. Sharing something so…"

Erin chewed her bottom lip. "Something so…what?"

"Awesome. Mind-blowing. Earthshaking. Take your pick."

She released the breath she was holding and laughed. "Yeah. It was all of those things, huh?" She slid a fingernail down his cheek.

Now Alec chuckled, and his laughter warmed her like the morning sun after a cold night.

Still grinning, he blew out a cleansing breath. "What a way to welcome the new year. Talk about fireworks."

Erin knit her brow, blinked. "New year?" She stopped and mentally calculated the number of days since her kidnapping at the end of Manny's knife. She shook her head in disbelief. "It *is* January first."

"Mmm-hmm. Which means we have five days to figure out what Daniel was onto and prepare for whatever's going down at the address in his notes on January sixth."

January sixth. Foreboding shimmied through her. Intuition told her something big would happen that day. Something dangerous. One way or another, by January seventh, she'd lose Alec.

Chapter 13

*N*ew Year's Day. Alec squeezed Erin's shoulder and kissed the top of her head. Regardless of his training, he had to say he liked the way he'd brought in this year far more than the year before. Last New Year's Day, he and Daniel had rung in midnight camped in a hovel in Colombia, sharing a cold can of hash and the end of the Kentucky bourbon in Daniel's flask. That was the life he'd been trained for. Not marriage and family.

So what the hell was he supposed to do now? He'd sorely underestimated the effect Erin would have on him. Making love to her had been explosive, decimating any objectivity or reason he had left in their relationship. Not good, considering they were still being hunted by killers. He still had a mandate, a job to complete.

"I need to study Lafitte's notes some more," he thought aloud. "See if he's left any more clues about what's going down in New Orleans in a few days. What he wants me to do."

"I've been thinking about it, too. I have a theory to run by you."

Alec nodded. Erin's instincts had proven keen earlier, but he had his own theories he had to investigate. Daniel was clearly feeding him information on a situation with enormous ramifications. A U.S. senator, his kidnapped daughter and the Colombian warlord he and Lafitte had been about to arrest when *someone* betrayed them. *Someone* who'd since tried several times to kill him. And he'd brought Erin into the middle of it.

Damn it. Rather than working to extricate Erin from the untenable position he'd put her in, by making love to her, by giving in to his feelings for her, he'd pulled her deeper into the mire. And what exactly did he feel for her? Was this *love?* How the hell was he supposed to know? He'd never allowed himself to care about anyone, never opened himself to anything like love. Not since his mom left. Not since he'd learned that love and loyalty were rare and hard earned. And easily betrayed.

No, he didn't love Erin. He couldn't afford to love her. Wouldn't allow himself to go down that road. He'd always been a good soldier, a good agent, because he didn't have personal relationships to jeopardize or distract him. He needed to reel in his runaway emotions and remember his priorities. His job was to keep Erin safe. To find Daniel and expose the mole in the agency, the person responsible for betraying him in Colombia.

Dragging his thoughts back to business, he tipped Erin's chin up for a quick peck on the forehead. "Isn't it about time to feed Little One again so you don't start feeling sick?"

"Little One says yes. You're really catching on to how this pregnancy thing works."

He grinned and swung his legs out of bed. "Considering I've seen you toss your cookies about half a dozen times if you didn't eat…"

Erin caught his hand before he slipped away and squeezed his fingers. "Just the same. It's thoughtful of you. Thank you."

Alec acknowledged her with a lopsided grin and shoved down the pang of regret for the could-have-beens that twisted in his chest. No matter how life changing, how spiritually awakening making love to her had been, he couldn't put her at more risk by allowing himself to believe their relationship was going anywhere else.

A few days later, as Erin watched Alec hover over a laptop and tap the keys, the blue-white glow of the screen lighting the masculine angles of his face, she tried not to think of the looming date. January sixth. Day after tomorrow. So little time left with Alec before—

"What the—?"

Alec's muttered surprise brought her from her musings. "Alec?"

"I have an email from Daniel. Encrypted." He was pounding the keys of his computer, his eyes locked on the screen.

Tossing the sheets aside, Erin hurried to the desk to peer over Alec's shoulder just as he unscrambled the email. The subject line read Epiphany.

"Listen carefully. Watch closely. Stick to the agreement. All is not as it seems," Alec read aloud. Daniel had signed the email with an L. Lafitte.

Then the email disappeared.

"Where did it go?" she asked.

"It was programmed to self-delete." Alec rocked back in the desk chair and stroked his stubbled chin, his expression troubled, contemplative.

"The essence of black ops," Erin said, her chest pinching with dread. "No records. No proof. Complete deniability." Was that how Alec would view their relationship in the coming months? Would he erase it, deny it happened, forget she ever existed?

"Epiphany," he mumbled.

"Like suddenly understanding something? Is that what he means?"

Alec swung the desk chair around to face her. "The date he scribbled on the pad."

Understanding dawned.

"Right." She nodded. "The day in the Christian calendar believed to be when the three magi reached the Christ child to present their gifts. So…what does the rest of it mean? What agreement is he talking about? What isn't as it seems?"

"Our agreement to put our missions first. Not to jeopardize a case. Every man for himself." Alec scowled, and a muscled jumped in his jaw. "He wants me to watch and listen. Set up surveillance equipment. Apparently he's not in a position to do so himself. Which means he's in trouble. Or being followed."

"But so are we."

"We were. He must think we've shaken our tail for now."

"What do you think?"

"I don't know what to think." He met her gaze, but she could tell he wasn't being completely honest with her. He knew something he wasn't sharing. "I know this, though. I'm not going to risk losing Lafitte again. Nor will I risk putting you in danger. When I go to the address Daniel left us on January sixth, I'll go alone."

She opened her mouth to argue, and he narrowed a chilling glare on her.

"It's not open for debate, Erin. You'll stay here. Where you'll be safe. It's the only way I can do my job without distraction."

Erin tensed. Stilled. The truth sank deep to her marrow, chilling her.

Despite the past few days of bliss with Alec, she was still an encumbrance to him, a complication, a hindrance to him working effectively and doing his job.

She nodded stiffly. "I understand."

Backing away from him, she pivoted on her toe and headed to the tiny bathroom for a cold shower. But the sting of the icy water couldn't be more sobering than the truth she had to face. She wouldn't lose Alec on January sixth. Because he had never belonged to her to begin with.

Chapter 14

Alec was dreaming. Of picket fences and vanilla-scented nights. Of contentment. Of commitment.

Until the tiniest of squeaks yanked him from sleep.

A floorboard. Someone crossing the room.

A click. Gun—

Even before his eyes opened, focused, Alec swung his arm toward the noise.

In an instant he knocked the attacker's weapon arm aside. The man's gun fired. The shot flew wide, splintering a plank in the roof.

Erin screamed.

Alec landed another lightning strike to the man's jaw. Their attacker stumbled back a step and aimed again.

"Get under the bed!" Alec shouted.

Jumping to his feet, Alec met the cold, deadly stare of his opponent. With a quick high kick, he disarmed the man. Lunged. As he grabbed the man by the shirt, shoving him against the far wall, a second man Alec hadn't seen wrapped a beefy arm around his throat from behind.

"No!" Erin wailed.

He heard the scrape of wood. A grunt and a thud. The hold on his throat loosened and fell away. With a quick glance over his shoulder, Alec spotted Erin wielding a chair and swinging at the second man. She caught the man broadside, and he went down, clutching his skull.

"I told you to get under the bed!"

"Alec, I—"

Alec's captive raised a knee to his gut. Breath whooshed from his lungs as pain spread through him. Mindful of the second threat and Erin's vulnerability, Alec acted quickly to neutralize the man in his grip. With an upward arc of his arm, he thrust his palm into the first gunman's nasal bone, jamming it into the cretin's brain. The man dropped like a wet rag.

"Alec, look out!"

At Erin's warning cry, Alec caught a reflection in the window of the second man's arm swinging down, a long blade flashing. With a duck and a roll, Alec dodged the knife. He swept his leg against the knifeman's legs and knocked him to the floor. Tackling the downed man, he seized him by the hair and locked his arm around his prey's neck. "Who sent you?"

"Santa Claus," the man grated.

Alec tightened his choke hold. "Who sent you?"

"Go to hell."

"Maybe someday. But you'll be there first."

Alec twisted the man's head until his neck snapped. When their assailant went limp, Alec released him and stood. His body shook with adrenaline—and fury. The men had threatened Erin's life, invaded the tiny corner of the world where he thought he'd found some peace, some refuge, some happiness.

But mostly he was angry with himself for allowing the attackers to get within striking distance. He should have sensed the intruders sooner, been on guard for a sneak attack.

He turned to find Erin and met her frightened eyes.

"Are you all right?" The question came out sharper than he intended.

Still clutching the wooden chair, she nodded, her skin pale and her eyes wide and bright with fear. She looked at the man whose neck he'd broken, then raised her gaze to him again. In her eyes he read shock, horror…disgust? She'd seen his deadly potential, his brutal skill and training firsthand now.

Alec's gut rolled. Was she thinking of the past several nights when his lethal hands had touched her? When he'd stroked her belly where her child grew?

She'd seen his dark side. How could she possibly want him, his ugly history and violent training in her life and her child's?

"I'm sorry you had to see that."

She blinked, tears filling her eyes, and shook her head. "If you hadn't, they…they would have killed us. You had no choice."

A different type of tremor raced through him then. Fear. Because the mere suggestion that something could happen to Erin, that he could lose her, that she could be killed because of the mess he'd gotten her mixed up in, filled him with an icy terror. Alec dropped his chin to his chest and exhaled harshly. "Why the hell didn't you get under the bed like I said?"

Defiance flared in her eyes. "I won't cower under the bed and watch them beat you to a pulp. Or worse," she cried, her voice shaking. "I had to do something!"

"I'm trained to handle situations like that. But if you'd been hurt, I'd never—" *Get the chance to tell you how much I care for you.* His throat closed as a swell of emotion choked him.

Erin stepped closer, reached up to stroke his face. "You'd never what?"

He pulled her against his chest and held her. Probably too tightly, but he couldn't seem to loosen his hold. The emotion and adrenaline pumping through him were a potent mix. "I'd never forgive myself." He shoved down the renegade sentiment and pushed away from her. "This changes everything."

"What do you mean?"

"I had planned to leave you here while I staked out the address in New Orleans. But now...this place isn't safe anymore."

Erin puckered her brow and sent him a dubious frown. "You think I should go with you?"

"No, you *shouldn't* be going! God only knows what will go down at this address tomorrow night. I don't want you anywhere near there. But after this—" he jerked his head toward the dead men on the floor "—I don't want you out of my sight, either. If they found this place, they could find you at a hotel or bus station or anywhere. I want you close, so I can protect you." He huffed his frustration, still shaking internally, knowing how close he'd come to losing Erin this morning.

Her expression grew uncharacteristically cool and detached. "I don't want to be in your way. You have a job to do."

True enough, but he didn't like the distant edge in her voice. The hurt.

His gut knotted, and he rubbed the pounding pulse in his temple. "We'll figure something out. I won't let you get hurt, Erin. I promise. No matter what, I'll get you out of this mess alive. You'll have your life back, the freedom to raise your baby without fear."

"Without you, you mean," she whispered, her tone frighteningly void of emotion. This cold, stoic Erin rattled him. Her eyes looked flat, lifeless.

"Yes," he grated, regret shredding his heart. "That's never changed. I never promised anything else. I—"

She held up a hand cutting him off. "I won't get in your way."

* * *

The silence in the rental car was deafening. After days of listening to Erin's chatter, Alec found her reticence this morning all the more worrisome. A cold winter rain added its pall to Alec's somber mood as they navigated the long interstate bridges over the marshy lands outside New Orleans.

"I'm going to stop somewhere in Metairie, so we can buy a change of clothes and some surveillance supplies," he said with a side glance. A small nod was her only response.

"Do you feel all right? Is it the baby? Should I stop for food?"

"I'm fine," Erin said and continued staring out the passenger window.

The monotonous *swish-swish* of the windshield wipers taunted him. *Look at her, Kincaid. You did this to her. You broke her heart, crushed her spirit.*

Guilt wrapped strangling fingers of regret around his throat. After seeing him snap the assassin's neck, she'd withdrawn. No, she'd been reserved even before that. Alec racked his brain, trying to recall what had triggered Erin's retreat. Even if he couldn't change anything about their situation, he didn't want to leave bad feelings between them. The fact that he was clueless about what he'd done to upset her simply proved his inexperience with relationships and how completely unsuited he was to give her the long-term happiness she deserved.

He glanced again at her bleak expression and muttered a curse under his breath. "I'm sorry, Erin."

She turned, her delicate brow drawn in a frown. "For what?"

Alec shrugged. "Hell if I know. Whatever I did to hurt you, to put you in this mood. You've hardly spoken a word since yesterday." He lifted a corner of his mouth. "That's not like you."

She sighed. "You haven't done anything. I knew days ago I was getting in too deep, letting myself feel too much for you. I've no one to blame but myself. You'd been up front all along that you didn't feel the same way."

She gave him a sad smile as she turned away, and his heart clenched.

"That's not exactly true." He gripped the steering wheel tighter, so hard his knuckles blanched. "I never said I didn't feel anything for you."

Erin's head whipped back around, confusion and a dim hope lighting her eyes.

Acid roiled in Alec's gut. He had to be honest with her. He owed her that much, by God. "I care very much about you. More than I've ever felt for anyone. I—"

I love you.

Moisture sparkled in Erin's eyes, and he jerked his gaze back to the road, unable to bear the pain and false hope he saw there. "But what I feel for you doesn't change who I am, what I am, what I have to do."

At that moment, if she'd asked him to quit the agency, take a new identity and leave everything he knew of war and terror and death behind, he'd have agreed in an instant. But she only bit her lip, nodding sadly, and turned back to the window.

Alec's lungs felt leaden, and the weight of his responsibilities suffocated him. As the edges of civilization appeared through the misty rain, he pulled out his training and forced all but the mission ahead from his mind. He had to stay focused. To screw up now could cost lives. His. Daniel's. Erin's.

A lightning pulse of fear skittered through him at that possibility, and he swore to do anything he must to protect Erin.

Stick to the agreement, Lafitte had said.

But he couldn't make that pledge. Because Erin's life and the life of her unborn child came first.

God help him. Sometime over the course of the past weeks, his priorities had changed.

After scoping out the Tchoupitoulas Street address from Lafitte's notes and confirming that the location was some type of warehouse, Alec parked the rental car in an abandoned lot a few blocks away.

Wearing her new set of dark blue sweats, Erin followed Alec along the riverfront, back toward the warehouse. Alec had changed into the long-sleeved black shirt and jeans he'd bought himself at their first stop on the outskirts of New Orleans. On his back, he toted a pack filled with all types of electronic gadgets, tools, tape and wires. Supplies to rig the warehouse with listening devices and tiny hidden cameras, he'd explained. But it was the bulge at the small of Alec's back that made Erin shiver.

His gun. At a gun shop, Alec had bought several more magazines of ammunition for his weapon and hidden a knife under the leg of his jeans. Both indicative of the violence he expected tonight. Erin shuddered and quickened her step to catch up to him, tucking herself close to him as a chill wind buffeted them.

With a brief glance in her direction, Alec slid his hand around hers and laced their fingers, anchoring her close to his side. The gesture was so unexpected, so sweet, that fresh tears burned Erin's eyes. She blinked rapidly to clear her vision and tried not to think of herself and Alec as an elderly couple, still in love and holding hands after decades spent together. She swiped at the drips of cold rain pelting her face and steeled herself against the grip of pain in her chest.

When they reached the warehouse, they found the door locked. Within moments, though, her superhero lover had gotten them past the flimsy security measure and, leading with his pistol, guided her inside the dim building.

"Stay here while I check it out," he whispered.

Erin rubbed the goose bumps on her arms and nodded. Despite the mild New Orleans temperatures, she couldn't buff away the chill that settled in her bones, in her heart. A cold sense of foreboding drilled her as she watched Alec sweep the warehouse with his weapon drawn, his flashlight skirting over row upon row of luxury boats stored in dry dock.

The cavernous building held a musty stench, and her every thudding heartbeat seemed to echo hollowly from the brick and steel construction. Tarp-draped yachts hung suspended or were shelved on moveable racks, one on top of another, row after row, from the damp concrete floor to the ceiling some sixty feet above. Watery daylight filtered in from a row of ventilation windows near the roofline. Dust motes danced in the thin light, and the hulking watercrafts cast black shadows in the recesses of the huge storage facility.

A large empty space had been left at the center of the warehouse, presumably to accommodate the movement of the forklift parked across the floor. A small steel desk and chair sat to the side of the door, and cockroaches scuttled out of sight when she swung the beam of her flashlight over the floor.

"All clear."

Erin gasped when Alec appeared from behind a concrete support pillar.

She pressed a hand over her runaway heartbeat. "Now what?"

He narrowed a concerned look on her, and she straightened her shoulders and raised her chin. She had to get a grip on herself, keep her head and do everything she could to help Alec, not hinder him. She glanced at the weapon he'd tucked back into the waist of his jeans and reminded herself of the stakes.

"I'm okay. I can do this. I want to help," she said, her voice much steadier than her nerves at the moment. She had to stay calm and think clearly. She could *not* get in Alec's way.

He gave her a reluctant nod. "All right. We're gonna wire the place. Get the pack."

When she handed him the backpack, she noted that his stern, all-business expression was in place. Grim. Taut. So far removed from the warm and generous lover she'd discovered recently that her pulse quickened.

The day had barely begun, and already she felt the man she'd fallen in love with slipping away.

"Check one, two," Alec muttered under his breath, then checked the tiny digital recorder's reception.

Check one, two, his voice echoed from the device.

"Okay, that's it. We're set." He nestled the wire-size microphone back in its hiding place by the light switch. "Now we wait."

"Wait where?" Erin asked, scooping up electrical tape and stowing it in Alec's backpack.

He turned his eyes toward the rafters. "Up there. C'mon."

Taking the pack from her, he grabbed her hand and started climbing a small set of narrow stairs to the first level catwalk. Erin followed, her heart in her throat as they traversed the steel grate and climbed to the next level. And the next. Higher and higher they climbed, while her anxiety mounted. When they reached the last level of catwalks, Erin prayed they were finished climbing. But they weren't.

Setting down the backpack, Alec grabbed the steel cable supporting one of the suspended yachts and leaped onto the deck.

"Alec?" she called when he disappeared inside the cabin.

"Wait there."

She did, her hands clammy and her breath shallow and fast as she peered down from the shaky catwalk to the floor five levels below.

When he reappeared, Alec had two nylon rope coils slung

over his shoulder and a mesh strap with carabiners attached in his hand. Much like the equipment she'd used when she'd gone rappelling with Bradley. She shuddered. "Alec? What—"

"Backup. Not that anything will happen, but…just in case." He jumped back across and the catwalk swayed and shimmied when he landed.

Erin gasped and grabbed for the thin railing. "Backup for what?"

He didn't answer. With deft hands, he lashed the straps, carabiners and rope together and held the contraption out for her. "Step in the loops."

Her stomach clinched. She recognized the harness configuration. A diaper sling, Bradley had called it. "We're… rappelling?"

He glanced up and crooked his mouth sideways. "No, sweetcakes. Backup, remember?"

"But—"

"I won't let you get hurt, Erin. I promise."

His promise reverberated in her chest, low and full of conviction.

"Step in the loops," he repeated.

Bracing one hand on his shoulder, she slipped her feet through the harness, and he connected the strap around her waist. Knotting one end of the rope through the carabiners at her hips, he tossed the other end of the rope over one of the steel rafter beams at the end of the catwalk.

"Where's your backup safety line?" she asked as Alec stepped to the edge of the iron-mesh platform where they stood.

He shrugged. "I work without a net." Then, before she could argue the point, he sprang across the four-foot gap to the I-beam support girder.

Once across, he looped and secured the rope and turned back toward her.

"C'mon. You can do it. Just like we jumped the rocks in that mountain stream."

A hysterical laugh bubbled up from her dry throat. "Need I remind you my dubious rock-jumping skills almost got you killed?"

A tiny grin cracked his stony facade. Warmth filled his eyes, and he stretched his hand farther out to coax her. "You can do it, Erin. Have faith in yourself. I do."

Have faith? She might not trust herself and her jumping skills, but she trusted implicitly the large, calloused hand he offered—the same hand that had intimately touched her, the same hand that had lovingly stroked her belly while Alec whispered words of affection to her baby, the same hand that had comforted her and calmed her fears numerous times in the past weeks. She trusted Alec with her life, with her heart, with her soul.

Extending her hand, she grasped his wrist, and with a giant leap, she launched herself across the empty drop to the floor.

Alec reeled her in close and steadied her on the narrow steel girder.

Instinctively she grabbed his waist, clinging as she shifted her weight to catch her balance.

"See?" He gave her mouth a resounding kiss. "I knew you could do it."

They continued jumping from one girder to the next, climbing, looping her safety line on the next support beam, until they were perched on the highest rafter in a dark corner of the warehouse. The juncture of joists and crossbeams and the steel plate to which they were all riveted made a tiny landing just big enough for the two of them to sit, hip to hip, their backs against the warehouse wall.

Alec knocked away a spiderweb and wrinkled his nose as he flicked the web off his fingers. He muttered something derogatory about spiders under his breath.

Despite their uncomfortable perch, Erin managed to catnap through the tedious afternoon of waiting and muscles cramping. The long hours stretched into the evening, until darkness engulfed the warehouse. Alec did his best to massage the ache from her limbs and fill the time with whispered conversation.

No matter how fatigue and tension wore on her, Erin refused to complain. She savored every moment of huddling on their high perch together, knowing the minutes could be her last with Alec.

"Promise me that no matter what happens tonight, you'll stay right here. You'll stay hidden. Stay safe. No matter what."

She couldn't speak. Apprehension clogged her throat, and fear for Alec's life left her mouth dry.

His eyes blazed, and he gripped her shoulder, gave her a shake. "Promise me, Erin. Or I'm getting you out of here *now.*"

She had no doubt he'd make good his threat and stash her in some obscure hotel or office building. But doing so might blow his chance to be in place when things went down at this warehouse. To witness whatever it was Daniel wanted Alec to monitor.

She bobbed her head once. Erin had sworn not be an inconvenience to Alec on this mission. If she couldn't help, then she'd fade into the background and stay out of the way.

But her answer didn't soften the intensity in his eyes. "If something happens to me," he growled, and she stiffened, swallowed a whimper of fear, "promise me you'll stay safe. When the danger's passed, go home. Go back to Cherry Creek and make a home for your baby. Be happy. Be strong. Don't waste a minute on second thoughts or regrets. Forget about me and move on with your life."

Her eyes watered, and she shook her head. "I can't promise that, Alec. I don't want to forget you. I never could."

His face darkened. "Erin, listen to me...."

She touched his lips to quiet him, and he sucked in a sharp breath. "No. I can't change the way I feel, Alec. I don't want to try. I—"

The thud of a car door closing outside echoed through the warehouse, stealing her breath. Stealing her chance to say anything more. They had company.

Chapter 15

Alec snatched the flashlight from Erin and shut it off. Darkness swallowed them.

He gave her fingers a final squeeze, then dropped her hand and shifted soundlessly away from her to watch and listen.

The warehouse door opened with a creak, and a man in a trench coat walked inside, leading with a handgun and sweeping the room with the beam of his flashlight. After a moment of investigating the scene, he flipped on the overhead light, and a bright glow flooded the warehouse. The man backed toward the door, then called outside. "No one's here yet, Senator. It's secure."

Senator? Alec glanced over his shoulder to Erin. Her eyes were wide and anxious.

Is it White? she mouthed.

An older man in a suit strode boldly to the center of the warehouse, as if he owned the place. A concrete support beam blocked Alec's view. He needed to move to a more central location if he wanted a clear line of sight.

Below him, the older man shifted restlessly and glanced around, his manner tense and edgy.

Alec squinted to get a better visual of the man's face. He turned back to Erin and nodded. Aiming a finger at her and drilling her with a no-nonsense look, he reiterated silently, *Stay here. Stay hidden.*

Without waiting for a response, Alec eased out on a cross-beam, staying low, moving quietly. Carefully, he inched across the expanse of the warehouse, over the heads of the senator and the half-dozen men who'd accompanied him, until he reached a center support. Hiding behind the concrete pillar, he had a bird's-eye view of the room. From the looks of the goons surrounding the senator, Alec surmised the men were private hired guns. Not Secret Service.

The senator paced, checking his watch. "Why aren't they here? I said 2:00 a.m."

"Perhaps you should wait in the car, sir," Trench Coat said.

"No, I want to be here when they arrive. Get this business done and get out of here," Senator White countered. "Did Grimshaw brief you about the terms tonight?"

"He said we don't give up anything until you have your daughter. When Ramirez releases Nicole to you, unharmed, only then do you give him what he wants."

Ramirez. Alec's senses slammed into overdrive. So there *was* a connection between the senator from Louisiana and the rebel Colombian general and the senator's daughter. Just as Daniel's sketch alluded.

"Precisely." White marched back to the center of the room and checked his watch again. "Your job is to make sure our bait doesn't show himself too soon."

Bait? Was this an unofficial prisoner exchange? Had Senator White been bypassing government protocol for finding his daughter by dealing directly with terrorists?

Alec checked the corner rafter to make sure Erin was still

out of sight. She'd sidled forward to watch the events below but was still protected by the concrete support. Erin met his gaze with a worried look, then shifted back into the shadows.

"What if LeCroix doesn't show?" Trench Coat asked.

Alec's pulse spiked. *Daniel.*

"He'll show," White said, and chortled smugly. "He's been tracking Ramirez for months. He'd never pass up an opportunity to net a fish this big. Besides, LeCroix thinks when this deal is done that he'll have his life back, that he'll have nabbed the man who put a bounty on his head."

The senator's adviser grunted. "He doesn't know that was you?"

Senator White pivoted slowly toward Trench Coat. "You think he'd have been working with me these past months if he knew the truth?"

A chill slithered over Alec's skin. Lafitte had been working with the senator?

Trench Coat shook his head. "I don't like it. It just seems too easy. You get Nicole back, while LeCroix and Ramirez each think you're turning one over to the other. They scrap it out and the strongest and smartest survives to—"

White swung around to face his adviser. "No one survives! Once I leave with Nicole, you and your men take care of both Ramirez *and* LeCroix. Ramirez dies for what he's put my daughter through, and LeCroix…because he's a loose end."

Adrenaline pumping, Alec prayed his recording equipment was picking up this wealth of information.

"What about LeCroix's partner? Kincaid?" Trench Coat's question snapped Alec's attention back to the discussion at ground level.

Senator White scoffed. "Kincaid is no longer a factor. By now he's gator food."

Fury and loathing flashed hot in Alec's blood knowing this man had put Erin's life in jeopardy in an attempt to kill him.

"He was hiding in the bayou?"

White nodded. "LeCroix helped us set a trap for him."

Across the warehouse, Erin gasped. In the hushed darkness, her sharply inhaled breath resonated like cannon fire.

Alec tensed, divided his gaze. Erin covered her mouth with both hands and shrank back into the shadow of the I-beam.

"Who's there?" The senator raised his head, scanned the rafters and suspended yachts. "You said the place was secure!"

Acid roiled in Alec's gut. He couldn't blame Erin for her reaction. If not for his training, he'd probably have had a similar, gut-level response to Daniel's betrayal.

"Search the place. Every last damn boat!" The senator swept an arm in a wide, angry arc.

Alec's muscles torqued tighter. Even a basic search of the premises would give Erin's location away. He'd been trained to hide anywhere, to become invisible. But Erin was vulnerable.

A niggle of uncharacteristic panic and foreboding grabbed him by the throat. Breathing became difficult. He'd die before he let anything happen to her. He had to stop the search. White had to think he'd found the source of the noise they'd heard.

Hoisting himself with the nylon rope, Alec rose from his hiding place. He tied the rope to the main joist and secured his grip. With a leap, he swung across to an I-beam one level below.

Pulling his SIG-Sauer from the small of his back, Alec eased out of the shadows and aimed his weapon on the traitorous senator. "Senator White, I believe you're looking for me?"

Erin bit her lip so hard she tasted blood. The metallic tang mixed with the bitter fear that rose in her throat. What was Alec doing? He'd be killed!

Senator White spun around and angled his head toward the rafter where Alec stood. The man's bodyguards whipped their weapons up, taking aim.

Erin swallowed a whimper and strained to listen to the unfolding scene over the thundering pulse in her ears.

With a raised hand, the senator warned his men to hold their fire. "Who's there?"

Nimbly, Alec slid down the nylon rope as far as it reached, then dropped the final ten feet. He landed smoothly, weapon ready. Poised and balanced. Like a cat.

Like a sacrificial lamb.

Tears burned her eyes. He'd given himself up to cover for her gaffe. Once again, a man she loved would die because of her. A primal cry of agony swelled in her chest, but she gritted her teeth to shove it down. She couldn't, *wouldn't* do anything to make matters worse for Alec.

She watched the man who'd sacrificed so much to guard her, who'd revived her faith in love and in herself, step into the circle of light where the senator stood.

"What's the matter, Senator? Don't you recognize the man whose execution you ordered? Half of the undercover team you sold out in your bargain with the devil?"

"Kincaid?"

Erin's heart kicked.

Alec smirked. "The goons you sent to the bayou didn't do their job."

Senator White straightened his shoulders and lifted his chin. He flicked an uneasy glance to the man in the trench coat, then back to Alec. "I suppose you heard about your partner's betrayal. Seems he had an axe to grind with you."

Alec shook his head. "Daniel would never betray me." He jerked his chin toward the gloating man. "Like you did."

White scoffed. "You're sure about that? How do you think I knew you'd faked your death with the plane crash in Colorado? Or the helicopter pickup in the mountains? LeCroix's been quite helpful in tracking you down in recent weeks."

If she hadn't known Alec so well, Erin would have missed the telltale twitch in his jaw. Did he believe the senator? Did something about the scenario the man painted ring true to Alec?

"But now that you're here," White said in a tone so low and menacing, Erin almost missed it, "I can be done with the both of you."

Keeping the gun trained on the senator, Alec narrowed his eyes. "Not if you want to see your daughter again."

The senator jerked. "What do you know about Nicole?"

"I know that you were willing to betray our covert op, your integrity and the United States in order to try to find her, save her."

White stiffened.

"I only recently came to understand that level of feeling," Alec said. "Love deep enough to make you forsake everything you ever believed about yourself…"

Erin caught her breath. Warmth expanded in her chest, and tears leaked from her eyes.

"I understand why you sold out, even if I can't agree with your methods."

The senator puffed out his chest importantly. "My loyalties to the U.S. are not the issue. I don't take kindly to being called a traitor."

"Then perhaps you shouldn't consort with known drug lords and terrorists or sell secrets concerning national security for personal gain."

"You can't prove anything!" The senator's voice trembled with rage. "I did what I had to to save Nicole, to get her back alive!"

"Oh?" Alec paused. "Do you really think Ramirez will bring Nicole tonight? He's smarter than that. She's his bargaining chip. Now, tell your boys to back off and put away their weapons, or I won't share what I know about Nicole."

Erin held her breath. What did Alec know about the senator's daughter?

Outside the warehouse, a car door slammed.

"Senator," one of the bodyguards called as he peered out the glass inset of the door. "We've got company."

Erin tensed. Watched the door for the new arrival.

The men below scrambled to take new positions, out of sight.

"Get him out of the way," the senator said with a flick of his hand toward Alec. "Don't kill him until we make the trade, and I know Nicole's safe."

One of the senator's men advanced on Alec. Erin opened her mouth to scream a warning, just as Alec swung around and landed a high kick that knocked the man's weapon from his hand. A second man tried to grab Alec from behind, but Alec spun and punched his new opponent in the gut.

Erin gripped the I-beam, watching helplessly, as Alec neatly handled each man that came at him. Her superhero knocked one guy out, slamming his gun to the back of the poor slob's head. Then he sent another guy stumbling back with a well-placed elbow to the chest. Alec held his own against the senator's bodyguards for several seconds. Until the guards organized themselves and ganged up on Alec.

Erin cringed. Her stomach bunched and rolled as the men brought Alec to his knees with brutal blows to his gut and chin. Duct tape was brought out to secure Alec's hands behind him.

Shaking all over, Erin shrank behind the I-beam for cover. She had to do something to help Alec. But what? Even Alec, with all his training and skills, couldn't overtake *all* of the senator's henchmen and their weapons.

The warehouse door opened with a loud screech of metal.

Erin's pulse thundered with dread. Her heart in her throat, she peeked around the steel girder to survey the unfolding scene.

A half-dozen Hispanic men strode into the warehouse carrying semiautomatic weapons. The senator's bodyguards visibly gathered themselves after their brawl with Alec and faced the new threat.

The scene reminded Erin of street gangs squaring off for a rumble. Finally, a Hispanic man garbed in a crisp business suit stepped inside and approached the senator.

Senator White leveled his shoulders and extended his hand.

The new arrival ignored the offer to shake hands. "Where is he? Do you have LeCroix?"

"And good evening to you, too, General Ramirez," White said, his tone dripping sarcasm. "Where is my daughter?"

Erin avoided gasping her horror by sheer willpower. Her reactiveness had already put Alec in an untenable position. She glanced to Alec, still crumpled on the ground, his hands bound. He raised his head and sent the Colombian general a dark glare.

Ramirez stepped closer to Senator White. "Your daughter is safe. For now. But I'm not a patient man. Either I get Le-Croix in the next sixty seconds or your daughter dies."

Visibly rattled, White lifted a conciliatory hand. "Let's not be hasty, General. I have something just as good as LeCroix. My men and I managed to root out LeCroix's partner." The senator signaled to his men. Alec was yanked to his feet, and his head snatched back by his hair. Erin's scalp stung with sympathetic pain, and her gut somersaulted.

She scrunched behind the protection of the I-beam and drew a slow, deep breath for composure. This was no time to lose control. Anger for their mistreatment of Alec fired a slow burn in her stomach. Love and admiration for the man who'd sacrificed himself to keep her safe and hidden swelled inside her until she couldn't breathe.

Above all, pain slashed through every other emotion and shredded her heart knowing without a doubt these men meant to kill Alec. The idea of living without him, of never having the chance to tell him she loved him, shattered her. She grieved inside, knowing her child would never know the courageous, honorable, loyal and loving man that had swept into her life, turned her world upside down and shown her what real love meant. An unselfish, undemanding love, unafraid of taking risks for the sake of another.

Erin felt her heartbeat stagger…slow to a crawl. *Unafraid of taking risks…*

Erin's pulse gathered speed again as a plan took form in her head. She wouldn't let Alec die without doing everything in her power to save him. He'd sacrificed so much for her and her baby, and she could do no less for him.

The voices of the men below her fell away as she searched her mind, scanned her surroundings, prayed. She couldn't rescue Alec alone, but she could get help, get the police. *If* she could get out of this warehouse undetected. She glanced down at the small army of armed men, a half-dozen or so from each camp, and knew she could never get out the way she came in.

Which left…

Heart thumping, Erin craned her neck. Eyed the row of ventilation windows near the ceiling. *Be strong. Be brave. Be resourceful.*

For Alec.

Determined not to admit defeat, Erin moved her gaze to the far end of the catwalk. Rebar rungs arced out from the wall in a crude ladder toward the ceiling. At the top, she spied a trapdoor, probably used by workmen who needed access to the roof.

Seeing no other way out, Erin sucked in a deep breath. Inching down the I-beam, she edged toward the ladder, the roof…and escape.

Alec ignored the pain shooting from his arms and his scalp as the senator's bulldogs yanked him to his feet. A subtle movement near the back of the warehouse snagged Alec's attention. He angled a wary gaze toward the catwalk while White and Ramirez stood toe to toe, daring the other to be the first to blink.

"Where's Nicole?" White demanded of Ramirez.

In the shadows near the back of the warehouse, a figure moved along the catwalk. A petite figure. Dressed in dark sweats. His breath hung in his lungs.

Erin inched to the edge of one of the boats suspended near the ceiling and leaped to the front deck. Where the hell was she going? He'd told her to stay out of sight!

Alec cursed silently, as the yacht swayed and creaked. Bile rose in his throat. If any of these men saw Erin, heard her clambering on the yacht…

A convulsive shudder raced through him at the thought of Erin being tortured or killed by these scum. He had to ensure that whatever Erin was up to, she wasn't seen.

"Don't be stupid, Senator," Alec rasped.

Both men swung their gazes to him. And away from Erin.

In his peripheral vision, he watched Erin climb out of the yacht and leap smoothly to the catwalk, a rope looped over her shoulder.

Alec forced training to the forefront, focusing on what he must do to save Erin, despite the swarm of angry bees stinging his gut. "Your daughter's dead by now. You've wasted your time with this little meeting."

Ramirez stiffened. The senator turned a pale and stricken stare toward Alec. "What do you know?"

Ramirez stepped closer to Alec, a vein in his neck bulging.

His arms still held by the senator's henchmen, Alec braced for the assault he knew was coming. The rebel Colombian general hadn't risen to power because of his clemency with traitors.

"You! You and your partner nearly ruined my operation," General Ramirez barked.

Alec gave the man a cocky grin. "Still will, if I have anything to say about it."

Ramirez landed a hard slap across Alec's jaw.

Ears ringing, Alec used the abuse as an excuse to move his head, flick a glance to check Erin's progress. She'd paused at the sound of the slap, and Alec's heart slowed.

No! Go. Keep moving!

Ramirez cast a quick glance to White before returning a black beetle-eyed glare to Alec. "He lies. I gave orders that your daughter wasn't to be touched until I returned." Snapping his heels together, Ramirez spun back to face the senator. "You cannot believe this *gringo!*"

"Then why isn't she here? I—I was supposed to get her back tonight!" Pain and frustration flooded the senator's voice.

Adrenaline pulsed through Alec, and as the two men argued, he monitored Erin's progress up the ladder, out to the roof. To safety.

And Erin's life was all that mattered to him.

Gravel and tar bit Erin's hands as she awkwardly levered herself up on the roof of the dry dock warehouse. Taking a page from Alec's book, she'd scavenged the supplies she thought she'd need from one of the suspended yachts. Tossing the coil of rope off her shoulder, she dusted her hands and reached under her shirt for the heavy gloves she'd tucked in the waist of her sweatpants. She loosened the carabiners and web-strap harness still cinched around her legs, hips and waist.

As she'd ascended the ladder, she'd conjured the dreadful day she'd gone rappelling with Bradley, forcing herself to focus on the hours before her husband's tragic fall. She recalled the detailed instructions Bradley had given her about how to thread and knot the ropes, how to secure the carabiners, and how the intricate belay system of knots and counter weight worked.

She didn't have nearly enough of the proper equipment to truly rappel down. But to save Alec, she'd find a way to use what she had. Erin quashed the swirl of nausea that rose when she thought of the task ahead and steeled herself. She refused to let her fear be responsible for the death another man she loved. Alec had sacrificed so much for her, gone out of his way so many times to accommodate her, to rescue her.

Because he cared. She'd seen it in every kind gesture and tender moment of their lovemaking, every noble and courageous risk he'd taken on her behalf.

Even if she had to slide down the rope as she had in gym class years ago, she *would* get off this roof and get help for Alec. She would face down her anxieties, make this risky climb for him. Not because anyone had pressured or manipulated her, as Bradley had, but because she *wanted* to. Because she loved Alec more than she feared climbing down that rope.

Erin found a sturdy pipe in the rooftop air-conditioning system and threaded her rope around it. Tested to see if it would hold her weight.

Satisfied the pipe was a sufficient anchor, she poked one end of the nylon rope through the carabiner Alec had secured at her waist. Then, arranging the rope around her to suit the task, she donned the gloves and tossed the end of the rope over the roof's edge. Peering down to the street level, checking what was below, she gathered her composure with a deep breath. Five floors. Approximately sixty feet straight down the concrete-block outer wall of the warehouse.

Whispering a prayer, Erin gripped both the rope leading to the pipe and the other end that dangled down the side of the building. She squeezed the two ropes with a death grip as she walked backward over the side of the building. Feeding a little rope at a time through the carabiner, she inched down, her feet against the building, the harness around her legs and hips taut and straining. Upper-body strength had never been her forte. Her arms began to ache as she worked her way down. Hand under hand, walking backward. Five feet, ten. Fifteen.

Her heart thundered. Sweat beaded on her forehead despite the cool night air. She battled the urge to look down, certain she'd freeze if she did.

One step at a time. Slowly. Another foot. And another.

Her untrained muscles quivered and screamed from exertion, and her hands throbbed despite the gloves. Down she crept, keeping her focus on just the next step, the next few inches of rope. Twenty-five feet. Thirty. Almost there.

A car horn blasted in the distance, and she heard someone laugh several streets away.

No. No distractions. Focus.

She sucked in a deep breath, grunted in pain and strain as she battled her shaking arms for the last ounce of strength to shimmy down the last few feet.

Erin gritted her teeth and dug deep in her soul for the will and the determination to hold on despite the burning in her muscles, the white-hot pain that speared her shoulders.

Alec. You have to do this for Alec.

One more step…

Erin's hand, sore and quivering with fatigue, slipped. She lost her balance and scrambled to find her footing. Her heart pumped a fresh dose of adrenaline. With a renewed spurt of energy, she clenched the rope, caught herself before she fell. But the jerk on her arms tugged a shoulder muscle already strained to capacity. A slicing pain shot up her neck, down her arm.

Her grip faltered again. Too weak to grab the rope a second time, she felt herself fall.

Colors blurred. Blood roared in her ears. Erin braced for impact with the concrete below.

Instead, her back hit a hard chest. Strong arms caught her around the waist. Those same arms supported her when her knees buckled in relief.

When she tried to turn, tried to see the face of her savior, the cold kiss of steel met her temple.

The click of a gun cocking reverberated through her skull. "That's far enough, sweetheart."

Chapter 16

"If you don't want a bullet in your brain, you'll put your hands on your head and turn around. Nice and easy," a deep voice growled.

Ice seeped to Erin's marrow.

"Please," she choked out hoarsely, pivoting slowly.

Alec. She had to get help for Alec!

"Don't shoot. I can explain—"

The midnight-black eyes and grim slash of the man's mouth stole Erin's breath.

Dressed in a tight black T-shirt and well-worn military fatigues, the man held his gun on her while his free hand skimmed impersonally down her waist and legs.

"I'm unarmed. I swear."

He grunted and continued patting her down.

"Please! Let me go…." She struggled for air. "Th-they'll kill him…. Need help…."

The deadly intent the man exuded should have scared her spitless. But something about his efficient movement, his broad shoulders and incisive gaze seemed familiar.

His hand stopped on her taut, rounded belly, and he lifted his coal-black gaze to hers. He said nothing, but one dark eyebrow lifted as he studied her. The gesture was so like Alec's, a flutter kicked to life in her chest.

"Daniel?" she whispered.

The man tensed. Narrowed his eyes. Retraining his gun on her temple, he grated, "Who are you?"

Doubt flashed through her. Senator White had said Daniel betrayed Alec. Yet Alec's faith in his partner hadn't wavered. Or had it?

"I-I'm with Alec," she said, trusting her instincts. "I'm a friend." A puddle of tears blurred her vision, and she blinked rapidly to clear her view. "Daniel, I need your help. Alec needs you."

The gun slipped, and the rigid set of the man's jaw softened. "You're with Alec?"

Erin nodded, warm moisture leaking to her cheeks. "He's been looking for you, searching everywhere. He got your letter. Actually, I got it, but I gave it to him. He found the map." Her words spilled out as relief and hope gushed through her. She'd found Daniel!

"And we found the articles, the notes about Senator White at the house in the bayou. That's why we're here. We knew you led us here because you needed help or something. White said you'd set Alec up, set a trap, but Alec didn't buy it." She knew she was prattling but couldn't seem to stop. Her explanation rolled from her tongue, carried by nervous energy. "We know about the deal Senator White made with Ramirez, and how he sold you out. But Alec—" Her breath snared in her throat. "Please, Daniel, you have to help him!"

His expression darkened again. "Where's Alec? What's happened?"

"He let the men see him. He took them all on even though he was outnumbered."

Daniel's brow puckered, and he shook his head in disbelief. "No, Alec would never—"

She grabbed Daniel by the front of his shirt. "The senator's guards overpowered him! They're holding him hostage, and—" Erin's voice cracked, and more tears spilled on her cheeks. "They're g-going to kill him!"

Daniel's scowl deepened. "Why would Alec show himself and ruin the operation when he was outmanned?"

Erin gave a hiccupping sob. "To save me. I made a noise, and they heard me. They'd started a search and…Alec surrendered himself. As a diversion, I'm sure. To stop the search. He offered himself up in my place." She felt the tension that hummed through Daniel's wiry, athletic body. She knew from the way he appraised her, then shifted his gaze to the warehouse, that Daniel's mind was clicking, calculating even as she explained her culpability.

Erin swiped away the tears that poured down her face. "I can't let him die because of me, because of my mistake." Clutching Daniel's taut, muscled arms, she poured her heart and soul into her plea. "Help me save him, Daniel. Please!"

Daniel's chiseled face hardened again, and his gaze snapped with purpose. "Is the baby you're carrying Alec's?"

Erin raised her chin, stunned by the question. Why did the paternity of her child matter now? "No."

Her answer seemed to surprise Daniel, but he nodded and gave the warehouse another careful scrutiny. "All right then," he said, drawing her by the arm out of the alley and toward the street. "Let me take it from here. You've already done more tonight than any woman in your condition should." He hailed a passing cab and pulled a wad of bills from his pocket. "Alec wanted you to be safe, so stay safe. Don't make his sacrifice be for nothing. Understand?"

Erin opened her mouth to argue, but Daniel grasped the center front of her throat and pinched. Hard.

She gasped her shock and tried in vain to wrench free of his hold. But darkness closed in from the edges of her vision. Her head grew heavy. Then a black oblivion sank over her.

Alec fought the darkness that settled in his heart. He had to believe that Erin was safe or he'd go crazy. Right now, he had to give his full attention to the two powerful men waging a war of bravado under his nose. A war likely to land him in the crosshairs.

"Enough waiting. We go," Ramirez said, stalking toward the door.

Senator White straightened uneasily and raised a hand. "Wait! LeCroix will be here. I'm sure of it." White sent Alec a meaningful look. "Because we have something he wants."

Ramirez snarled reproachfully. "You have nothing. This one left LeCroix for dead in the jungle."

Acid and guilt gnawed Alec's gut, and he raised a cool glare to Ramirez.

The general snapped his fingers and crooked his head toward the door. His men readied to leave. "*That* is how these men work." He raised his index finger and waved it. "Only *numero uno*. LeCroix will not come for Kincaid."

"Not even for revenge?" White taunted. "LeCroix's the one who told me how to find Kincaid. He brought Kincaid out of hiding and delivered him here tonight."

A thread of doubt wound through Alec and pulled, cutting deep. Could it be true? He'd known someone inside the agency had compromised his location in order for White's men to have sent the pickup chopper and set their trap. But Daniel?

No. He refused to believe it. Daniel would never sell out.

Ramirez strode back to Senator White. "Perhaps you were the one who was duped. I wanted LeCroix. You failed to deliver. Our deal is off. Your daughter will die." Ramirez spun on his heel and stalked toward the exit. He gave a nod toward Alec and barked to his men, "Kill him."

Alec's gut pitched. Where was Daniel? More important, was Erin safe?

"Wait!" White shouted to Ramirez's retreating back.

One of the rebel soldiers aimed his Uzi at Alec.

A loud pop ricocheted in the warehouse. When the soldier with the Uzi fell, confusion erupted among the ranks. The tension in the warehouse ignited.

White reached inside his suit coat, drew a pistol and leveled it at Ramirez. Immediately, the general's men fired. White's guards returned fire.

Chaos reigned. Curses shouted. More shots.

Hands still bound, Alec tucked his head, rolled behind the aluminum desk near the door. He lifted his gaze to the rafters, searching. And found the man he expected.

Daniel.

Knife drawn, his partner slid down from the catwalk using the same rope Alec had used earlier. In two steps, Daniel reached Alec, then grinned at his friend. "Perfect timing as usual, Lafitte."

Daniel sliced the tape at Alec's wrists. "I met your lady friend outside."

"Erin? Is she all right?"

One of Ramirez's soldiers grabbed Daniel from behind.

Daniel ducked his head. Alec smashed his fist in the soldier's nose, and the soldier slumped to the floor.

Daniel snatched out a pair of handcuffs. "She's safe."

"It's LeCroix! Stop him!" White shouted.

Alec exchanged a look with Daniel that said all he needed to know. He had his partner back, and it was time to get to work.

Taking the Uzi from the fallen soldier, Alec crouched low and headed for the warehouse door. No one was leaving the scene on his watch. As Daniel dispatched one of Ramirez's men, Alec took out the thug firing from the hull of one of the suspended boats. The exchange of gunfire continued in a confusing barrage. He wanted the senator and Ramirez alive, to stand trial for their crimes. He swept a shrewd gaze around the warehouse and spotted Senator White skulking behind a stack of crates to avoid the volley of bullets. Across the room, Ramirez stepped out from behind a concrete pillar and leveled a pistol.

Daniel appeared behind the general like an apparition. With a tug on Ramirez's arms, Daniel handcuffed the general to the same concrete post the man had used for cover.

For a split second, Daniel's eyes met Alec's.

The general was captured. Alive. Mission accomplished.

Then Daniel's arm shot up. Lafitte pointed his gun.

Toward Alec.

A pounding throb in her head pulled Erin out of the black fog around her. Blinking, she took in her surroundings. A vehicle of some sort. It was moving.

A taxi.

She struggled to sit up, rubbing a sore spot at the front of her throat. And remembered.

Daniel had used some strange pinch hold to knock her out. She straightened in the seat with a gasp. *Alec!*

Erin rapped on the partition between the back and front seats. "Stop! Stop the car!"

The driver shook his head. "I'm sorry, ma'am. Your friend paid me a lot of money and told me to deliver you to a hotel where you would be safe. He took down my driver's number and swore to come after me if I didn't do as he said."

Her friend? That remained to be seen. Could she trust Daniel?

Her driver made the sign of the cross and shook his head. "I don't want that man with devil's eyes to come after me!"

She banged the partition again. "Please, stop! I have to get help for Alec!"

"*Non,* ma'am. I cannot."

Erin pressed her palms to her pounding temples and tried to think calmly. What would Alec do? Her heartbeat stuttered when she considered her best option—bailing from the moving cab. As it had in the warehouse, when she'd first considered her daring escape, a niggling fear wound through her. But her love for Alec, her fear for his life, silenced the doubts and bolstered her courage. The only thing she wouldn't risk for Alec was her baby's life. Anything else was fair game. Alec was her heart, her soul mate. She knew that now with certainty.

Glancing out to the dark city streets, she watched the historic buildings of New Orleans flash by her window. As they approached town, the cab slowed to make a turn, and Erin recognized the opportunity. Prepared.

The next time the taxi slowed for traffic, Erin popped the door handle and leaned into the door.

"Ma'am!" the driver shouted as she jumped out of the cab and stumbled to the curb.

Without a backward glance, Erin ran. She searched the storefronts as she hurried past, searching for a business that was open. She needed a phone. Fast.

Finally, at a twenty-four-hour laundromat, she found one of the last of a dying breed of pay phones and snatched up the receiver. Her first call was a brief one to 911. After reporting the crimes at the warehouse and making sure the police and an ambulance were dispatched, she hung up.

She had another call to place. With shaking hands, she paged through the tattered phonebook hanging by a chain below the pay phone and found the number she needed. The office of Senator White.

As expected, she reached an answering service.

"I need to speak to someone on the senator's staff immediately. It's an emergency!"

"Emergencies should be referred to the police, ma'am," the operator said.

"I've called the police. But Senator White is at risk, and I must get a message to him. Now!"

After a brief pause, the operator asked her to hold.

"This is Ralph Godwin, Senator White's chief of staff. May I help you?"

"Yes. You can give the senator a message." Erin pressed a hand to her stomach and fought the wave of nausea swirling there. She had only to think of Alec, the man she loved and a hostage of the traitorous senator, to firm her resolve. "Tell Senator White that I know about his deal with Ramirez, how he jeopardized two undercover American agents and betrayed his country."

"What are you talking about?" the man on the line asked.

Erin felt sure the senator's chief of staff knew exactly what she meant. "Tell the senator that if Alec Kincaid is harmed in any way, I will go to the press, to the FBI, and shout his crimes to anyone who will listen."

With her emotions running high, adrenaline pumping through her veins, Erin was confident she could follow through on every one of her threats if anything happened to Alec.

"Who is this?" the chief of staff barked.

"Tell the senator I have proof of what he's done, and that if he wants to find his daughter, Alec Kincaid had better be released immediately."

She slammed down the receiver before the stammering

man on the other end could reply. Erin shook, inside and out. She'd laid the groundwork. Now she could only pray her plan worked.

Alec stared down Daniel's muzzle for a splintered second. Then he dove, twisting as he rolled, and aimed the Uzi at the man Daniel had spotted behind him.

"Freeze, Senator!" Daniel barked.

White paused, turned. The man raised his hands and faced Daniel with a defiant glower.

Lafitte's returned glare was lethal, determined. Alec lowered his weapon. Daniel had earned this one.

"You're a traitor to our country," Daniel grated. "A disgrace to your office."

White stiffened and narrowed his eyes. "So shoot me. What are you waiting for?"

Alec furrowed his brow, curiosity plucking at him as he watched the emotional battle that played across his partner's face.

White backed toward the door, and Alec tensed, waiting for Daniel to take his shot. Around the warehouse, silence testified to the extent of Ramirez's and White's fallen or unconscious guards.

White took another step toward the door.

Sweat beaded on Daniel's brow. His hand flexed and tightened on his weapon.

"Lafitte?" Alec shifted, uneasy with what he witnessed.

White gave an oily smile and turned the knob on the warehouse door. "You're the best black ops soldier our country has?" the man scoffed. "Killing you would have been a favor to the nation."

When White opened the door, letting the damp cold of the night inside, Daniel fired. White crumpled, clutching his leg, howling in agony.

A muscle in Daniel's jaw jumped. "I'll let the police and the press handle you. Your days as a free man, much less a senator, are numbered."

Alec released the breath he held and turned with a grin to Daniel. "Well, partner, looks like we—"

Daniel lobbed a right hook and caught Alec in the chin. Alec stumbled back and fell on his butt. Rubbing his offended jaw, he raised a stunned look to his best friend. "What the hell's that for?"

Daniel aimed an accusing finger at him. "You almost cost me nine months of deep-cover and ass-breaking work!" He stepped closer and towered over him, his dark eyes blazing. "What possessed you to come looking for me? Every man for himself. Remember? What happened to your training?" Daniel's tone scathed and abraded Alec.

Sucking in a slow, deep breath, Alec searched his soul for a way to answer his partner. He'd asked himself the same question so many times in the past days with Erin. People were the priority, even at the cost of a mission.

Perhaps he'd realized as much months ago when he'd started his search for his partner, even if he hadn't been able to call his understanding by name.

He met Daniel's accusing glare evenly. "You're my partner...and my best friend. My only friend. How could I *not* try to find you?"

His answer clearly startled Daniel. Alec grinned, knowing how Daniel felt. Some of the things he'd learned about himself were shocking to Alec, as well. "Besides, I knew you'd do the same for me."

Daniel blinked, arched an eyebrow and gave him an arrogant look. "Oh? Think so?"

"I know so."

The whoop of sirens and strobe of police lights filtered in from outside. The cavalry had arrived.

The corner of Daniel's mouth curled up, and he offered Alec his hand. "Still a cocky, overconfident son of a gun, I see."

Alec took Daniel's hand and let his partner help him from the floor. Once on his feet, Alec tugged Daniel's arm, pulling him into a bear hug. "Yep. Some things never change."

Erin was a mess. Her emotions, spiked by pregnancy and adrenaline, were all over the map. Her clothes were dirty and tattered. She'd cried so hard in the past hour, her eyes had puffed until she could barely see.

But nothing would stop her from getting back to the warehouse, getting back to Alec and finding a way to help him. She jogged down the dark streets of New Orleans, praying another cab would come by, but not waiting. She'd run the whole way if she had to.

Alec. Please, Alec, be all right!

Had Daniel been in time? Could he be trusted? It would kill Alec if Daniel had betrayed him. Like his mother had.

Pain slashed a deep swath in her soul. More than anything, she wanted to give Alec the acceptance and loyalty he'd been denied all his life. The *love* he'd denied himself.

If he'd only give her the chance.

Her body ached from her descent from the warehouse and her lungs hurt from exertion, but she put one foot in front of the other, over and again, until she merely stumbled along the narrow city streets. Finally, by heading toward the river, she found Tchoupitoulas again.

As she staggered around the corner and glanced up and down the deserted street, wondering which way to turn, an ambulance screeched by, sirens wailing. It turned a couple blocks down, where the strobe of flashing lights lit the night.

Heart in her throat, Erin staggered to a run. She covered the short distance to the warehouse quickly and rounded the building to the back where the emergency vehicles were parked.

She arrived in time to see a body bag loaded in the back of the coroner's van. Bile rushed up her throat, and she gagged. Spun away. Threw up.

Not Alec! God, please!

The ground beneath her wavered, and she clawed her way back into control. *Hold it together, Erin.*

"Ma'am? Are you all right?" She felt a hand on her arm. "You shouldn't be here. This is a crime scene and—"

"Where's Alec?" she rasped, cutting off the policeman at her side. "Is Alec all right?"

"Who?"

Before she could explain, the warehouse door opened with a loud squeak. Men's voices filtered through the night, and Erin turned, searching for...

"Alec!" she cried when his tall, dark form separated from the others.

His head came up, his gaze finding her. She saw Alec mouth her name, his shoulders rise and fall on a deep sigh.

Her own body trembled with relief, and her weary muscles gave out. She sagged against the policeman, and he caught her elbow before she toppled.

She blinked away the sting of happy tears and only then realized Alec's hands were cuffed behind him. A policeman shoved him toward a waiting patrol car.

"No!" Reenergized by the fear that swamped her, Erin surged forward, breaking free from the policeman's grip and running toward Alec. "Stop! You can't arrest him! He did nothing wrong!"

The cop who'd helped her caught her arm again and brought her up short. "Stay back, ma'am."

"No!" She struggled against his hold, gaining a few inches, but still a car's length separated her from Alec.

"Erin, don't," Alec called, and she froze. "It's all right. I'll talk to the authorities and straighten things out. They're just doing their job."

She swallowed the lump in her throat, nodded. Alec would straighten everything out. She flashed him a brave smile. "I'll get the rental car and meet you at the police station."

"No."

Her smile faltered. *No?*

The cop behind Alec tugged his arm, nudging him toward the patrol car. When Alec said something over his shoulder, the cop paused, gave a jerky nod.

Erin waited, her breath suspended in her lungs. "Alec?"

He lifted his gaze to her, his eyes flat and barren of the emotion she'd seen the past several days. Her heartbeat stumbled, and a cold ball of fear knotted her gut.

"Go home, Erin," he grated. "Go back to Colorado. You're safe now. You don't need me anymore."

She knitted her brow, sure she'd misunderstood. "You're wrong. I'll always need you, Alec. I…I love you."

He winced, sucked in a harsh breath as if she'd struck him. His jaw tightened, and his gaze hardened. "Don't do this. Just…go."

"No!" Her voice shook, a counterpoint to the trembling that started deep in her core and soon engulfed her whole body. "I want to stay with you. I want—"

"It's over, Erin. You're safe, and you need to go home. Forget about me."

Fingers of panic clawed at her chest. "What about us? What we have—"

"Is over. There is no *us*. There never was." A muscle in his jaw twitched, and he heaved an exasperated sigh. She searched his face for some telltale flicker of emotion, some crack in his stony facade. But found nothing.

"I don't have time to argue with you, Erin. I told you from

the beginning I couldn't give you what you needed. Nothing's changed. I have a job to do, and you have a child to think of."

Her blood pounded a desperate rhythm in her ears, and she fought to stay in control. "It can work, Alec. I know it will mean sacrifices on both our part, but if we love each other—"

"I don't love you, Erin."

Erin staggered back a step, her knees buckling. Only the policeman at her elbow kept her on her feet. She stared numbly at the man she'd given her heart to.

I don't love you, Erin.

The ground seemed to shift, and a viselike grip squeezed the breath from her lungs.

"Go home," Alec repeated. Firm. Cold. Unyielding. "Take care of your baby, take care of yourself and…" He hesitated, squared his shoulders, and balled his hands into fists. "Have a good life."

With that he turned toward the patrol car and climbed into the back seat. The cop slammed the door closed, and the thud echoed hollowly through Erin's breaking heart.

Chapter 17

Alec avoided Daniel's curious look as he climbed in the patrol car next to him. When the door slammed shut, he flinched, the sound jarring with its finality.

He stared straight ahead, yet saw nothing but Erin's grief-stricken face in his mind's eye.

His heart beat a slow, guilty cadence in time to the strobe of police lights in the predawn darkness. Feeling the weight of Daniel's steady gaze, Alec closed his eyes, seeking the refuge of the black void. But still images of Erin flashed before him, shredding what was left of his wounded heart. Erin jumping from an airplane with him. Erin kissing him amid the falling mountain snow. Erin matching wits with him as they deciphered Daniel's map.

And Erin making love to him while her gentle spirit and generous heart made him love her.

As the police car pulled onto the street, he released a shuddering breath and dropped his chin to his chest.

"Coullion."

He raised his head when Daniel spoke and shot his friend a puzzled look. "What?"

"It's Cajun," Lafitte said blandly. "It means you're an idiot."

Alec scoffed. "Gee, thanks."

"Just call 'em as I see 'em."

"I don't want to talk about it." Alec glanced out the window as the grillwork and ancient brick of downtown New Orleans flashed by his window.

"She loves you. And it's pretty damn clear you love her, despite that little speech. That heartless 'I don't love you' crap you threw her," Daniel said, his tone sharper now. "What was that? Are you insane? Why would you throw away something like that?"

"I don't want to talk about it!"

Daniel shook his head in disgust. *"Coullion,"* he muttered, shaking his head, growing silent again. For about ten seconds. "Do you know what she was doing when I found her? Huh? Rappelling down the side of a flippin' five-story warehouse!"

An odd combination of pride and pain arrowed through Alec. Erin rappelled. For him.

Daniel gave a short, humorless laugh. "The woman climbed down a rope from a warehouse roof. To save *your* sorry hide. When I found her, her arms were so tired and shaky she couldn't even hold on to the rope. She fell."

Alec snapped a worried look to Daniel. "What?"

"I caught her. But she could have been hurt. Seriously hurt. And the baby... She's pregnant, for cripes' sake! Do you have any idea the sacrifice she made for you? The risk she took to help you?"

"More than you have any idea." An image of Erin at the mountain hideout, crying and shaking, overwhelmed by memories of Bradley's death, shook Alec to the marrow. His chest constricted.

"She did it because she loves you." Daniel grunted and scowled. "But that means what to you? Nothing? *I don't love you, Erin,*" he mimicked in an ugly tone.

"Stop it!" Alec snarled.

"She deserves better than that," Daniel snarled back.

"Damn right she deserves better! Better than me! Better than the kind of life I can offer her. Better than the danger she'd be in by association with me. Hell, you know the kind of jobs we do, the kind of scum we deal with every day. What kind of life is that for her? For her child?"

"So leave the team! Take a job at the post office."

Alec fell back against the seat as if Daniel had punched him. "Leave the team?"

"Did I stutter? Yeah, *quit.* Do something else."

Alec frowned, his mind staggered by the possibility of walking away from his job. "But this job is who I am."

"Bull, it's what you *do.* It's not your identity."

"But it…it's all I *know.* Since the time I was on the streets as a kid, it's all I've ever known. Fighting. Survival. Danger."

"Then I'd say you were due a break, buddy. A little peace."

Peace. Alec thought of the quiet calm that settled in his soul when he'd shared his past, and his heart, with Erin. The contentment he'd known lying next to her, the bliss of making love to her. For the first time in so many years, he'd felt he had a home. That he belonged.

But he'd sent her packing. For her own good. He was not the kind of man she needed cluttering her life, putting her at risk.

So leave the team! Alec scowled.

Right. Leave black ops work and then what? Where would that leave him?

Before Alec could consider the answer, the patrol car pulled up to the police station.

He knew the drill. Cooperate with the cops. Reveal nothing. By midmorning, high-level government officials working with the black ops team will have cut through legal and bureaucratic red tape. Alec and Daniel would leave the police station as free men. Just as they had numerous times before.

Through the windshield, Alec watched the cops unload one of Ramirez's men from the car in front of them. Most of the senator's and rebel general's other men had been killed in the frenzy of gunfire. Trench Coat was in custody and being questioned.

White and Ramirez had been taken to the emergency room under heavy guard to be treated for their gunshot wounds.

Alec sent Daniel a side glance. "Ramirez in the U.S. That was a surprise."

His partner shrugged. "Not the first time, it turns out. He kept close tabs on his drug operations here. Came in under the radar with his junk." Daniel shot him a wry grin. "DEA had a fix on him. We stepped on some toes tonight, no doubt."

"But he and White are in custody. That's what matters."

And Erin was safe.

That alone should give him a sense of closure. Of a job completed. Mission accomplished.

But it didn't. He'd handled things with her badly. He knew that. Compunction grated through him as their driver and his partner stepped out of the vehicle.

As soon as the officers closed the front car doors, Daniel shot Alec a glance. "You wired the warehouse. Right?"

"Roger that."

"Will the uniforms find anything when they search the building?"

"I'll be sure they know where to look."

Daniel gave a terse nod. "White or the general give anything up?"

"Plenty. Enough to fry White for his involvement." Alec eyed his partner. "So there was no mole in the agency? It was you the whole time, feeding White and his hired guns intel on where to find me, what my next move would be?"

"I knew you could handle yourself, that you'd put the pieces together and do the right thing. I needed White to believe I was working with him in order for this whole op to fall into place." A look of guilt passed over Daniel's face. "I didn't know you had Erin with you."

Alec gritted his teeth. "So White is the one who sold us out to Ramirez? The fiasco in the jungle was a setup to draw us out? A setup that leaked to some of Ramirez's other enemies?"

"That's about the size of it."

"Then why'd you balk with White, Lafitte? What's going on?"

Daniel blew out a breath, and his expression hardened. "Seems White has been keeping track of me for years through his connections at the Pentagon."

"Keeping track of you? Why?"

"Let's just say we have history."

"Meaning?"

One of the policemen approached the patrol-car door.

"Later."

"Does it have anything to do with Nicole?"

Daniel snapped a startled gaze toward him. Alec tugged up a corner of his mouth. "I'll be damned. Erin was right."

Before Daniel could voice the question in his eyes, the back doors opened and the officers hauled them both out of the patrol car.

Alec's questions regarding his partner's intentions toward White's daughter would have to wait.

Three weeks later

"I have a few questions about your involvement in the death of Joey Finley." Harvey Bines, the principal of a new private elementary school near Cherry Creek, folded his hands over his chest and gave Erin a hard look.

In response, she squared her shoulders and met the man's querying gaze levelly. "Yes, sir. What would you like to know?"

In the weeks since she'd returned home, she'd had plenty of time to reevaluate her life. Her marriage to Bradley. Her career. Her future with her baby.

And her time with Alec.

His rejection had sliced her to the quick, yet everything had happened exactly as he'd told her it would. He'd never promised her a future, never said he loved her.

The first several days after returning from New Orleans, she'd barely been able to get out of bed, mourning her loss. Missing Alec. Worrying about him.

After a week of feeling sorry for herself, she'd realized wallowing in self-pity couldn't be good for the baby. She had to pull herself together and move on. Her time with Alec had taught her a lot about herself, her capacity to love, to grow, to rise to a challenge.

The principal's mention of Joey Finley stirred a lingering sadness, but no longer caused shards of guilt to immobilize her.

"Joey's parents blamed you and your unorthodox teaching method for the boy's death," Bines said.

Erin took a slow breath. "I know that, sir. But what is so unorthodox about trying to encourage a child who feels he's a failure? Joey suffered from poor self-esteem. I wanted him to believe in himself and to know that I had faith in him. Given the same situation, I'd do it again."

Mr. Bines raised an eyebrow.

"That's not to say I'd use stories of my skydiving experience for motivation again," she added quickly. "That much I do regret, and my students' welfare will always come first. But, sir, I have learned that all fear and regret can do is immobilize you. Hold you down. Real courage comes from love, from faith. If you believe in yourself, you can accomplish more than you ever imagined."

She paused, hearing Alec's words the morning after his tumble in the frigid stream. *You were grace under pressure and did everything exactly right. I think you're going to be a terrific mother.*

Warmth spread through her chest. "I will not apologize for encouraging kids to be their best. We all make mistakes, sir. And we can either learn from our mistakes and grow, or we can let the fear of repeating our mistakes paralyze us. I choose growth."

Bines rocked back in his chair, clearly surprised by her answer.

Erin wiped her palms on her skirt. She wanted this job desperately, wanted the chance to teach again, to prove herself, to move on. But if she didn't get this job, she'd try again elsewhere. She wouldn't give up. If nothing else, Alec had taught her to have faith in herself. She'd treasure that gift from him as she treasured every memory of their time together.

"Well, Ms. Bauer, I have to say, you've impressed me. You are our strongest candidate to date." Bines stood and extended his hand. "Thank you for coming in. I'll let you know what the board decides."

She offered her hand, thanked him and made her way out to her car, more hopeful than she'd been in months.

A gentle snow was falling, reminding her of her first kiss with Alec. Bittersweet memories buffeted her, and she tugged her coat closed at the throat.

The baby gave a kick, and savoring the sweet thump, she patted her tummy softly. "Yeah, sweetie, I miss him, too." She sighed and slid into her car. "Let's go home."

Alec sank down in the leather couch of the mountain bunker and leaned his head back to stare at the ceiling. He tried not to think about how different the safe house felt without Erin there.

Memories of her were everywhere—the couch where he'd held her, the bed where she'd slept, the kitchen where they'd heated chili to feed her growing baby. If he closed his eyes, he could even imagine he still smelled vanilla in the air.

Cripes but he missed her! How was he supposed to forget her and move on? Knowledge of how he'd hurt her suffocated him. He was drowning, and painful regret weighted him down like too much ballast on a sinking ship.

Pinching the bridge of his nose, Alec groaned.

"For God's sake, Blackbeard. Should I just shoot you and put you out of your misery?" Daniel's chair at the computer console creaked as he swung away from the screen.

"That'd be too easy. I deserve to suffer for hurting Erin."

Daniel scoffed. "Instead of playing martyr, why don't you come take a look at what just came through from the agency."

Alec shoved to his feet and crossed to study the computer screen over his partner's shoulder. William Manny's face filled the screen. *Knife.*

"Seems the info you provided on William Manny and his partner was enough for the police in Seattle to track them down and arrest the both of them for kidnapping and attempted murder, among other charges. You don't need to worry about those thugs going after Erin to silence her."

"Thank God for that." Alec sighed and turned to pace.

"So when are you going to admit you were wrong and find

Erin?" Daniel swung his chair around to face him. "Talk to her, Alec. Fix things with her."

"Talk? About *what* exactly? Nothing's changed. Her life is homemade meatloaf in the suburbs, and mine's canned hash on the run in the jungle. I can't be the man she needs."

"That's crap and you know it."

Alec shot his partner a scowl.

Daniel spread his hands palms up. "You are the most universally competent man I know—next to me, of course." He gave Alec a smug grin before sobering and adding, "You're a genius at getting past even the tightest foreign security. But I also know the look you get in your eyes when we walk through a native village, when you see the women with their children."

Alec shifted his feet uneasily. "I get a look?"

Daniel nodded. "Man, I know you had it rough as a kid. I know your mom bailed on you."

Alec tensed, not liking the direction of this conversation.

"What's more," Daniel added, "after five years of slopping through the mire with you, I can read you like an open file. The thing you want more than your next breath is the one thing that scares the crap out of you. Home. Family."

A prickle ran down Alec's spine. He thought of the tender moments he'd spent with Erin, his hand on her belly, listening to her dreams for her future with her baby. He'd allowed his mind to picture himself beside her before reality had intruded and shattered his illusions.

Daniel's expression mellowed. "Family life is the one thing you don't know. The one area where you have no training to fall back on. You hate going into something with no plan, no expertise, no backup."

Alec's legs grew rubbery, and he sank on the sofa, numbed by Daniel's assessment. Because Lafitte was right.

"Maybe you even think you don't deserve a family like

everyone else. Maybe your mom's disappearing act screwed with your head, made you think you were unworthy somehow."

Alec's mouth became dry, and he felt the blood drain from his face. Lafitte always had been an excellent marksman. But Alec didn't like having his private pain, his psyche, as Daniel's target. Not when his partner was so dead-on accurate.

Daniel didn't relent. He leaned forward, propping his arms on his knees, and drilled Alec with an unflinching candor. "Alec, she loved you enough to face her deepest fears. You told me how her husband's death had scarred her. But she was there when you needed her. She rappelled off that building for you." He paused, scratched his chin. "Good thing, too. If she hadn't warned me what I was walking into, things inside that warehouse might have gone down much differently. She saved both our asses, really."

Daniel pushed to his feet, strolled into the kitchen and took down the bottle of scotch. He splashed the amber liquid into two glasses and gave Alec a hard look. "God knows you've been the best partner I could've asked for. But the writing is on the wall. I think you've earned your retirement from the agency. I think you have a new career ahead of you…as a family man."

Alec stared through the windshield of the delivery van at the house where he'd lived for eight short months. A lifetime ago.

But it had never felt like home. Not for him. Yet the last time he'd been here, to pick up Daniel's letter, he sensed a warmth and peace inside those same four walls the minute he stepped over the threshold. Erin had managed in a week what he hadn't in eight months. She'd made the house a home.

A hollow ache pressed against his ribs, and he swallowed hard. He started to climb out of the van then hesitated.

What would he say? Where did he begin to explain all the tangled emotions in his heart?

Alec slipped his gun harness off his shoulder and locked it in the glove box. He didn't want any reminders of his violent past around when he begged Erin for a fresh start, a second chance.

Before he lost his nerve, Alec strode up to the front porch, a bouquet of wildflowers in his arms, and took the steps three at a time.

Before he could knock, the door flew open, and Erin greeted him with a tearful gaze. "I think you have the wrong address."

He flashed her a tentative smile. "I hope not. The card says they're for the woman I love."

She raised a trembling hand to her mouth. "Love?"

"I need to say how sorry I am for hurting her. And that I was hoping she'd give me a second chance. Does that woman live here?"

"But that night…at the warehouse you said—"

"I know. Forgive me. I needed you to believe I felt nothing, so you could move on with your life. Problem was, I found I couldn't move on with mine…not without you in it." He laid a hand on the bulge at her belly, more pronounced now than three weeks ago. His breath snagged in his throat. "You and the baby."

Tears filled her eyes as she took the flowers from him, and he hurried on with his explanation, terrified she'd shut him out, send him away. "The thing is…I was afraid of loving you."

"Afraid?"

"God, yes. Loving you scares me to death, sweetcakes."

"Wh-why?"

He forced a laugh. "Come on. Marriage, diapers, mortgages and car pools. That stuff is terrifying to a guy like me."

"But you're a black ops agent…."

"No." He framed her face with his hands and whispered, "I'm a guy who has never had any semblance of a home life or family before."

Erin's face crumpled, and a tear broke free of her lashes. "Oh, Alec, I should have realized—"

He placed a finger over her lips. "Be my family, Erin. You and Little One."

"But what about your work? What about the danger we'd be in?"

"I'm leaving the black ops team."

She shook her head in confusion. "To do what?"

He shrugged. "I have options. I can train agents. Be a recruiter. Join the police force. I have enough in savings to float us for a long time while I decide what I do next."

She grinned. "I have no doubt you can do anything you want to do."

He swallowed hard and drilled her with an imploring gaze. "What I most want to be is a husband, a father, a family man. With you."

Erin opened her mouth, and he heard a tiny hitch in her breath.

"Erin, I love you. More than I've ever loved anyone or ever *will* love anyone. Marry me. Grow old with me. Have *my* baby."

She blinked, her expression stunned. "I don't know what to say."

He grinned. "That's gotta be a first."

She gave him a hiccuping laugh as tears spilled from her eyes. "Yes. My answer is yes! I would love nothing more than to grow old with you and hold hands with you when we're ninety."

Laughing his joy and relief, Alec sank his fingers into her thick vanilla-scented hair and pulled her close for a deep kiss.

Eleven months ago, he'd launched a manhunt for his best friend in the jungles of Colombia. But in searching for Daniel, he'd found so much more than he ever dreamed possible.

He'd found his happiness. His soul mate. He'd found his home.

* * * * *

COMING NEXT MONTH from Harlequin Romantic Suspense®
AVAILABLE JUNE 19, 2012

#1711 HER COWBOY DISTRACTION
Cowboy Café
Carla Cassidy
When Lizzy Wiles blew into town, she never expected a handsome cowboy to capture her interest...or that someone wanted her dead.

#1712 IN THE ENEMY'S ARMS
Marilyn Pappano
As a humanitarian trip to Cozumel turns deadly, there's only one person Cate Calloway can turn to: her longtime enemy Justin Seavers.

#1713 AT HIS COMMAND
To Protect and Serve
Karen Anders
Lieutenant Commander Sia Soto is on a collision course with danger. Only the sexy man she left behind can get her out alive.

#1714 UNDERCOVER SOLDIER
Linda O. Johnston
Sherra Alexander is shocked when her purportedly dead high school sweetheart appears in her apartment—and now he says she's in danger.

You can find more information on upcoming Harlequin®
titles, free excerpts and more at www.Harlequin.com.

HRSCNM0612